THE GOOD GIRL

ASHLEY ROSE

❀ Created with Vellum

FOREWORD

Want to be first to hear about specials on Ashley Rose books? Sign up for her newsletter
https://www.subscribepage.com/ashleyrosebooks
and receive the exclusive epilogue to her young adult mystery, Raven.
You'll also be the first to know when each book in the Pacific High Series is available!

1

———

Hunter and I are getting hot and heavy in his Jeep outside my house when my phone dings. I pull back and glance down.

It's a text from my mom.

"She just boarded."

"Cool," he says.

My mom is taking a red eye from New York. I'm going to skip school to pick her up in the morning.

Her text reminds me of what Hunter and I have both been trying to avoid talking about all night—the fact that we're going to court tomorrow to see if Josh Masters is going to be held on charges of attempting to rape me.

Josh has been out on bail since shortly after it happened in December. I've been a nervous wreck since then. He got kicked out of school but nobody really knows where he is. The entire football team at school seems to hate me. Josh was one of their best players. They always give me dirty looks and make comments when I walk by alone.

Luckily, Hunter makes sure I'm hardly ever alone. At school or after.

During the preliminary hearing on Friday, Hunter testified that he came up on Josh pinning me down on the beach attempting to rape me. But then Josh's attorney asked for time with the judge and when they came back out of chambers, the judge said there was a new witness who would be testifying on Monday.

Later, the district attorney told us who it was.

Ava Bradley.

My sworn enemy.

I'm a nervous wreck about what she is going to say and do. And while I'm beyond excited to see my mom, it's overshadowed by my nervousness about court tomorrow.

"Try to get some sleep," Hunter says kissing my brow. I open the door to go inside, all my desire vanished, morphed into apprehension.

Even under ordinary circumstances, a text from your mom while you're making out with your boyfriend is a definite buzz kill.

2

Oscar is already awake when I stumble into the kitchen in the pre-dawn darkness. I woke late. He's dressed and ready to go. I'm in baggy sweats and a tank top, but quickly change into the clothes I'd set out the night before. Oscar had taken me shopping to pick them out for my court appearance: a black pencil skirt, black heels, a black silk shirt. I wonder if my mom will even recognize me if I'm not wearing shredded jeans and my signature black boots. At least I talked Oscar into letting me stick to an all-black outfit. I wanted to feel like myself even in a situation that would be foreign and terrifying.

My mom's plane lands in an hour.

I can't wait to see her and hug her as tight as I can. It almost takes the edge out of the fact that I'm going to see Josh Masters in person today. I hadn't seen him since police led him away in handcuffs only moments after he'd attempted to rape me. If it wasn't for Hunter yanking Josh off me and beating the crap out of him, my entire life would be different right now.

Josh had threatened to press charges against Hunter for assault and battery but had apparently dropped the idea. Probably on the advice of his attorney.

After we pull out of the driveway, Oscar suggests we drive through for coffees.

"Yes, please," I say. I know I shouldn't have caffeine because it will make me even more nervous, but I didn't sleep well last night.

That doesn't stop me from sucking my latte down on the drive to the airport. Oscar is surprisingly quiet and subdued, which I don't mind. He plays some old 1980s station on the radio and I'm glad we don't have to talk.

At the airport, I'm searching every face that comes through security until I see her. Her curly black hair is shining and she has on pink lipstick and her eyes are sparkling. I choke back a sob. She looks great. For once her skin doesn't look ashen and she doesn't have bags under her eyes.

She is using a cane, but she's walking on her own. When I left Brooklyn. She'd been barely able to use a walker.

I race over and hug her so tight I can't breathe. She buries her face in my shoulder and we both weep.

I hear a woman nearby say, "Airports are so sad."

But I'm not sad. These are happy tears.

We finally draw back and my mom holds my shoulders at arm's length. "Oh, baby, I missed you so much."

I don't trust myself to speak so I simply nod and swipe at my wet face. At least the tears have stopped.

Then my mom turns toward Oscar and hugs him. "You are an angel sent from heaven," she says and he grins.

The three of us head toward baggage claim grinning like fools.

It's only later when we are in the Hummer again that I remember why my mom is here.

But she soon distracts me by asking endless questions.

"I want to know everything. I want to meet this Hunter. Oscar approves and that says volumes," she says. "And your girlfriends? Will I have time to meet them? If not this trip, then I'm coming back for spring break."

"I can't wait to introduce you to everyone!" I say.

"Oh, good!" she says. "And Oscar, you promised to take me to a fancy restaurant."

"Damn right," he says. "Tonight, or tomorrow for sure. Meanwhile, let's grab a bite to eat somewhere not so fancy before we head to court."

Court. It's like a black cloud suddenly swoops in over our sunshiny morning.

"I'm starved," my mom says. She gestures to the black slacks and beige blouse she's wearing with flat ballet slippers. "By the way, is this outfit appropriate?"

I know she's talking to me and I flush with shame. I remember the past few years I'd always bitch about her clothes and how she could make the effort to dress more stylishly but didn't bother. I was such a dick. I had no idea at the time. Stupid hormonal teenager. And here she was trying to basically keep our family from falling apart because of my asshole dad.

"Of course!" I say. "You look beautiful, mom."

And I mean it.

I wish we weren't spending most of her visit in a courtroom dealing with—I almost said the worst day of my life—but it wasn't the worst day of my life. Sadly, my dad gave me that already. Attempted rape was awful, but didn't rank up there with the horror of seeing months of abuse culminate in my dad's arrest and my mother being injured so badly she had to have surgery while I was in the waiting room praying that she would live.

Nope, thanks to my dad I've possibly already experienced the worst day of my life.

Unfortunately, my mom is only going to be here two days. She is enrolled in an accounting class and is worried about missing too much school.

We talk about that over eggs at some trendy place disguised as a dive. But I spot at least two celebrities at tables. Oscar always knows the hottest spots. My mom is telling us about her accounting class.

"As soon as I get certified, I'll be moving out of the place I'm in," she says. Then she turns to me. "Do you like your new school?"

I smile. "I do. I really do."

"Even with what happened?" She says it very carefully and takes a bite of toast while I answer, chewing and keeping her eyes on my face.

"Yes. I'm not going to let him ruin my senior year." I look her right in the eyes so she knows I'm serious.

"That's my girl," she says.

"But I really miss you," I say. I've been denying it to myself until now. But now that my mom is here with me, I realize all the hurt I've been holding onto. All the desire for a mom to hug and wipe away my tears when I have a bad day. The truth is I haven't had that mom for a few years because she was so beat down from my dad, but I see her here again.

"I miss you, too," she says and pauses. "I've been thinking … if it's okay with you, I'm going to move out here, too."

"What?" I set down my orange juice glass.

"Is that okay with you?" she asks tilting her head.

"Yes!" I say so excitedly that Oscar smiles and then mock scowls.

"Geez, and I thought you liked living with me," he says in a teasing voice.

I blush. "I love living with you."

He laughs. "Kidding."

"I just need to get my certification and then work a little to save some money to get a place and then I'll be there."

I can feel the smile slip from my face. I look down to try to hide my disappointment. It's going to be a long time before she can move here.

By the time that happens I'll be in college, which seems so far away. The only reason I can even go to college is when my grandma died a few years ago, she left me money in a trust specifically for college. Now I wonder if I can just use it to help my mom move here. I'd rather work and get scholarships for college if it means my mom is nearby.

Oscar clears his throat. "This may not be the best time to discuss it because we should really get going," he says. "But I've already thought about this a lot and wanted to bring it up: my entire downstairs is set up as a separate suite. There are two bedrooms with baths, a living room, a galley kitchen and a private entrance."

"What are you trying to say, Oscar?" my mother says.

"Justine, I think you should move in while you get on your feet. As soon as you get certified, why don't you come out and then stay with me as long as it takes to get established as an accountant out here and get some money saved?"

"Mom?" I say and all my hopes are on that one word.

"Besides, if Kennedy goes away to college it's going to be lonely for me," Oscar adds.

My mom laughs. "You'll never be lonely, but I might take you up on the offer, that is very generous."

As we walk out, Oscar turns to me, "Just in case you think I'm offering charity, Kennedy, you need to know that this offer I'm making your mother is actually a very, very long overdue pay back."

"Oh, Oscar, you know there is no pay back in question."

I raise an eyebrow, sensing a good story coming.

3

"When we were in high school," Oscar says as we walk to the car. "My dad kicked me out of my house when he found out I was gay."

"That's terrible," I say, frowning as we get in his pink and white Hummer.

"I was living on the streets for a couple days until your mom decided I should sneak in to her house and live in the basement."

"What?" This surprises me. My mom is such a rule follower. "Grandma didn't know?"

My mom shakes her head. "Nope. She never went in the basement because of her bad foot."

"Your mom made a bedroom down there for me and snuck me food every day," Oscar says meeting my eyes in the rearview mirror.

"Cool."

"But then your grandma found out," my mom says and they both laugh.

"I liked Wheaties and your mom hated them. When your grandma noticed boxes and boxes of the cereal were disappearing, she got suspicious."

"Boxes and boxes?" I say.

"Have you met a teenage boy?" he asks. I think of Hunter and how he will pour an entire bag of chips into a bowl and eat it in one setting.

"Good point."

"When your grandmother confronted me," my mom says, "I couldn't lie. I had to tell her what I'd been doing for five weeks."

"You lived secretly in nanna's basement for *five weeks*?"

Oscar nods.

"What did nanna do when she found out?" I ask. My nana was a little crabby and quite strict. "Were you grounded for the rest of your high school life, mom?"

My mom laughs. "Nope. When I told her she just stared at me and told me we'd talk after school and for Oscar and me to come straight home."

"I was scared shitless," Oscar says.

"I bet," I say.

"When we walked into the house after school, my mom didn't say a word, just started walking down the hall and looked at us like we were supposed to follow her," my mom says. "She stopped in front of her sewing room and held the door open. We looked in and her sewing machine and quilting stuff was all gone."

"Instead," Oscar interjects, "there was a twin bed with brand new bedding. A little wood desk and a bookshelf. And there were new clothes in the closet."

"You're kidding?" I am astonished. My crabby tight-fisted grandmother did all this?

Oscar shakes his head. His eyes meet mine again in the rearview mirror. His are bright with tears.

"Not that he would've ever worn anything she picked out," my mom says. "I mean this was the 80s so Oscar wore pink polo shirts and pegged jeans and my mom had picked out tan slacks and button down checked shirts..."

"Hey, I wore them sometimes," he says. "Just to make your mom happy."

"Yeah, but you changed as soon as we got to school."

"So, wait," I say. "You lived with my mom and nanna?"

"Until I graduated and got a job as a best boy on movie sets out here."

"Wow," I say.

By this time, we are at the courthouse. They've done a great job distracting me with this story. I guess you never really know someone. I will always look at memories of my nanna in a new light.

We climb out of the Hummer and head for the entrance. My phone dings. It's Hunter.

"You here?"

"Just pulled up."

"I'm outside the court room."

"See you soon."

4

When we turn the corner in the hallway, I see Hunter and stop dead in my tracks.

Holy shit. That hot guy killing it in a black blazer, tight black T-shirt, and slacks is my boyfriend. I can feel my cheeks grow hot.

My mom looks at me and then back at Hunter.

"He's pretty easy on the eyes, isn't he?" she says and winks and my face feels even more flushed.

He's pacing and looking around nervously. His longer black hair is slicked back and his eyes seem bluer than ever with him dressed all in black.

I can tell right when he sees me because he freezes and a slow grin spreads across his face. He takes me in, from my high heels to my pulled back hair and his smile grows wider.

When we get closer, I'm cursing my tendency to blush. But as soon as we walk up, he walks over confidently and sticks his hand out to my mother.

"It's such a pleasure to me you, Mrs. Conner."

She seems so little next to him. She smiles back and says. "Nice to meet you, Hunter. Thank you for looking out for Kennedy."

I wince at her words, even though I know they are well intended.

"My pleasure," he says.

Before we can say more, the courtroom door is opened by a bailiff and we file in.

My heart is in my throat. This is really happening. Oh my God.

It all feels surreal. As the judge takes other cases, the district attorney handling my case comes and sits beside me. She points to the court docket on her phone, showing that my case is coming up soon. Then she stands and talks to someone else in the back of the room.

Hunter reaches over and squeezes my hand. My other hand is clutching my mother's hand. I'm starting to have a panic attack. Everything feels surreal. I can't breathe. I gasp for breath. I'm starting to get dizzy.

Wildly, I glance around the courtroom for Josh and am relieved I don't see him anywhere.

But I see Ava sitting there. The bitch is dressed in an all-white body hugging dress and high white pumps. Her blonde hair is pulled back in a neat ponytail and she has pearls on. And here I sit all in black.

Jesus Christ. If you stood us side by side she'd look like the angel to my devil.

"What the hell is she doing here?" I say in a raspy voice. "Doesn't she have to stay outside the court until she's called?" Hunter turns and then scowls.

"Bitch," he says in a whisper as he turns back around. Then he seemed to remember my mom is right here and he looks horrified. "Sorry," he says to my mom.

My mom smiles. "Kennedy has told me about her. I think that is a fairly accurate word to describe her."

Meanwhile, seeing Ava here has pushed me over. I feel as if I'm going to vomit or have my breakfast come out the other end or something if I don't get out of there right away. I even start to stand but my mom pulls me forcibly back down.

"Don't let her win," my mom says in a low voice.

But I don't know if I can do it. I don't know if I'm strong enough.

Hunter leans over and says in my ear. "Just breathe. You got this. I'm right here."

I feel the panic clawing at my throat and want to get up and run out of the courtroom. But Hunter keeps talking. "Breathe in with me," he says and inhales deeply. "Now out."

I concentrate on his words and try to mimic his breathing until I feel calmer.

The panic subsides and I release my death grip on my mom's hand.

When the judge calls our case and the district attorney gestures for me to follow her into the area in front of the judge, I think I might actually be able to do it.

"We are just waiting for Mr. Masters to arrive. He still has thirty seconds until he will be held in contempt of court."

Hope fills me until the door in the back of the room opens and Josh walks in.

I whip my head back around to face the judge but not before my eyes pass over Hunter in the front row sitting with my mom and Oscar. He takes in Josh with a look that sends a chill down my spine. I know right then that if he could, Hunter would murder Josh with his bare hands.

It's a terrifying realization.

Then I'm facing the judge. I can feel Josh's eyes on the back of my head as he walks toward the front. I know people say that, but I swear it is real. I feel his stare to my very core and it makes my shaky confidence fly out the door. I can't do this.

The district attorney leans over and smiles and says, "You are a brave woman. Don't forget that. And don't forget the point of this."

I told her when we first met that the only way I'm going to be able to do this is because I want to make sure Josh never does this to another person again. Before he did this to me, he did it to others. And got away with it.

I can feel Josh come sit at the table to the side of ours. The judge holds his hand over the microphone and says something. The district attorney and Josh's attorney go up to speak to the judge in low tones. I can feel Josh's eyes boring into me.

"Quit look at her, fuckface." It's Hunter. I turn and see Josh's head swivel behind him. He gives Hunter a smile and licks his lips. Hunter jumps out of his seat and Oscar and my mom are holding him back when the bailiff rushes over.

"You're out of here."

"But I'm testifying," Hunter says.

"You can wait in the hall," the bailiff says. "Pull a stunt like that again and you'll be held in contempt of court."

I watch the bailiff holding Hunter's arm walking him toward the back of the room and out the door.

My heart is racing now.

The district attorney comes back to our table. She is frowning and my heart sinks.

"There is some new evidence. A video tape. That's what the new witness is going to testify about. We're going to go view it in chambers."

If there is evidence of the attempted rape—which is the only evidence I can think might exist— why is she frowning? I don't have a chance to ask her because Ava is in the front of the room now and my attorney stands and disappears with the judge and Ava holding her Super 8 camera. You've got to be fucking kidding.

After about thirty minutes, a bailiff comes through a door leading to the back rooms of the court and announces that court is adjourned until that afternoon.

Josh's second attorney walks out of court with him. I don't move until the door closes behind them. Then I rush over to Hunter and my mom and Oscar.

"What do you think's going on?" I say, my voice shaking.

Hunter lifts his phone. "I've been asking around," he says. "It's not good."

"Let's go talk somewhere privately," Oscar says. "I know a place."

We pile into the Hummer and go to a coffee shop a few blocks away. It's only when we are seated that Hunter says. "From what I heard Ava has been bragging that she has video footage of that night showing it was consensual."

I scoff. "That's impossible." But I also remember standing at the bonfire and having her point her camera at me. And the red filming light was on.

"What do you think that could mean?" My mom asks Oscar.

"It depends. I mean this is where the judge decides whether there's enough evidence to hold Josh over for trial on the charges," he says.

Unfortunately, the evidence isn't that great. It's basically my word against Josh's. Even though I went to the hospital with scratches on my face, there was no physical evidence of sexual assault.

And Hunter's testimony was considered iffy anyway, the district attorney said, because Hunter had beat the shit out of Josh so badly. Josh had a broken nose, black eye and broken ribs. It would not go over well in court even if he explained he had been saving me from Josh.

I'm worried.

When we head back to court I soon find out I'm right to be worried.

When we walk in and head to the courtroom, the district attorney is waiting for me.

"I'm so sorry," she says. "The judge dismissed the charges."

"How is that even possible," Hunter says, his voice raised.

She takes us to her office to explain. Ava had footage of me and Josh kissing and me smiling at him and then she had additional footage of us out by the water with him kissing me. It ended before it showed me trying to get away or throwing me on the ground.

And then she had extended footage of Hunter beating the shit out of Josh while I sat on the sand and watched. It looked like I had a smile on my face, but it was dark. There was no way I would be smiling.

"I'm sure you were crying, not smiling, but the light is so bad it's hard to tell."

Oh my God.

Before we leave, the district attorney tells me that all is not lost.

"When we met for the first time you told me that making Josh serve jail time for what he did was less important than making sure other people knew what he was capable of, right?" she asks.

"Yes," I say. I feel like I'm going to vomit.

"Now they know," she says. "He has an arrest record for sexual assault and was charged with sexual assault. Even though we lost this case, your bravery matters."

It doesn't feel that way, though.

It feels like I got punched in the gut.

5

Nobody feels like going to dinner that night.

I sit on the couch at Oscar's in my flannel pajama pants and a blanket over me eating pizza and watching a Will Ferrell movie with Hunter, my mom, and Oscar.

After the movie, I tell Hunter I need to go to bed. I'd been up early to get my mom.

I kiss him at the door without saying much and go climb in my bed.

The next day, Hunter skips school and shows up at my place at eight.

We are all up, but still in pajamas at the bar in the kitchen sipping coffee.

Hunter bounds in like an enthusiastic puppy.

"Let's go show your mom why she should move to L.A.!"

I know he's trying to cheer me up so I smile and agree.

Hunter offers to drive us in his Jeep and be the tour guide. Oscar is loving it. He sits in the back with me so my mom can see better. We start with the Griffith Observatory.

"This is where the famous scene in 'Rebel Without a Cause' was filmed," Hunter says, as we drive up to the planetarium.

"Cool!" My mom says. "I had the biggest crush on James Dean when I was little."

"As you should," Hunter says.

"Trivia tidbit," I say. "The first time I met Hunter in film class he was quoting James Dean."

He turns and looks at me after he parks. "You knew that was Dean?"

"Duh."

"We were meant to be."

"I also know you only quoted the first part of what he said."

He laughs. My mom turns and smiles at me. I can tell she's happy about me dating Hunter. I am so glad.

After that, Hunter takes us on his own personal movie tour: Union Station (Blade Runner); Randy's Donuts (Mars Attacks); The Frolic Room (L.A. Confidential); the Bradbury Building (Chinatown); and then spots such as the Hollywood sign and Mulholland Drive. We end at Mann's Chinese Theater and the Hollywood Walk of Fame.

We swoon over a few stars, such as Humphrey Bogart and Lauren Bacall and Johnny Depp. While Hunter takes selfies by Jackie Chan and Charlie Chaplin's stars.

Oscar runs over to buy us something to drink while we take selfies. I laugh. Of course, he's too cool to take any.

He is making goofy faces and then lays down taking a picture from above with his head on the star. When he stands, he looks past us and his face turns ghost white.

I whip my head and see a frail looking woman in a long, dirty skirt, and several scarves smiling at him and calling his name.

He backs up with his palms held out in front of him as if he is warding off evil.

"No. No. No," he says.

I look from him to the woman. Then it hits me.

She has the same blue eyes with ridiculously thick and black eyelashes. Except her eyes are bloodshot and yellowed. Her skin is spotted with sores. She's still beautiful in a strange, faded way.

Hunter's mother.

He turns on his heel and is gone around a corner at a loping pace before I can stop him.

I yell his name, but it's too late.

"It's his mom," I say in a low voice.

My mother looks at me and tears spring to her eyes.

The woman is closer now and gives a small, sad smile. "I just wanted to say hi to my boy."

She weaves on the sidewalk as if she is going to tip over. My mom is instantly at her side, holding her arm and leading her to a bus stop bench.

The woman puts her head on my mom's shoulder and cries. My mom pats her hair. "It's okay. It's okay," she says.

Suddenly, I'm angry with Hunter for running away and leaving us to deal with his mother.

My mom is talking to the woman in a soft voice. "I'm Justine. What's your name?"

The woman blinks as if nobody has asked her name in a long time.

"I'm Elizabeth."

"Nice to meet you, Elizabeth. Hunter's your son?"

The woman nods after a small delay.

My mom smiles at her. "You sure have a wonderful son. He's such a nice young man."

Elizabeth nods. "He is the only thing good I ever did. I was never a good enough mother for him."

Oscar rounds the corner with his hands full of drinks and his eyes widen.

I take him aside and explain. When he's filled in, he steps to the side and makes a call. Then he calls me over.

"I called Hunter's dad."

"What?"

"He needs to know. He's sending a car for her. He says he's been searching for her for months. She's been AWOL. He's got a spot reserved at a desert detox facility. They've been saving it until he could find her."

I nod. This is good. I'm filled with relief.

I text Hunter and fill him in.

His reply floors me.

"What? I can't fucking believe he called my dad."

I'm suddenly angry.

"Are you fucking kidding? He's only trying to help. Now your mom is going to get the help she needs."

He doesn't answer. I don't care. What a dick.

Unbelievable.

Within twenty minutes, which is record time in Los Angeles, a car pulls up to the curb. A man in jeans and a button-down shirt steps out and comes over to introduce himself to Elizabeth.

"I'm Chad," he says. "Mr. West sent me. He has a place for you to stay."

She doesn't argue and follows him over to the car.

She willingly gets in the passenger seat. She doesn't turn to look at us or say goodbye as my mom closes the door. As the car pulls away I see her slump slightly and press her face to the window.

It makes me so sad.

We spend the rest of the day at the beach and at a fancy restaurant until it's time to take my mom to the airport for her flight at ten. I don't hear from Hunter and I don't text him. He's being a child. I say as much at dinner, grumbling. Oscar and my mom exchange glances but don't say anything.

As I hug my mom goodbye at the airport's security checkpoint, she whispers in my ear. "Honey, don't be so hard on Hunter, his heart is broken."

I pull back and ignore her words, saying. "Mom, I can't wait until you move out here. I loved having you here. I miss you so much."

She smiles. "I know! I loved being here. Now I'm more motivated than ever to finish my class and get my butt out here."

I wave at her after she passes through security and then I stand there with Oscar by my side until she disappears into the crowd.

6

I decide to wait until the following week to go to school again. My teachers already have given me all my assignments this week online since we weren't sure how long the preliminary hearing would last.

Hunter doesn't text me until two days after my mom leaves. And when he does, his text pisses me off.

"Hey. Miss you. Want to come over and get busy?"

What the fuck? Why is he ignoring everything that happened? Why is he treating me like a booty call? What the hell. He didn't even bother saying goodbye to my mom. And he acts like we just saw each other an hour ago.

"I don't think so."

"Suit yourself."

Wow. I have to admit I'm slightly stunned. I thought he'd at least argue or ask why. But he acts like he doesn't give a shit.

At first I want to ignore him but my anger gets the best of me.

"How about this?" I text. "How about you explain running off on us and then not saying goodbye to my mom or texting me until now?"

I wait but he does not respond.

It's not until the next morning he texts back. I'm lying in bed waking up when I hear my phone ding.

"Sorry. I was drunk."

I am barely awake but I feel the anger surge through me again.

"Wrong answer," I write. "What the fuck is your problem Hunter?"

My phone rings.

"What?" I say, not bothering to hide my irritation.

He doesn't speak at first.

"Your mom is great," he says. I wait, but he doesn't say anything else.

I finally cave. "That's all you have to say?" I say.

"It's really hard to be around her."

"That makes no sense," I say.

"You saw my mom, Kennedy."

I pause for a second to find the right words.

"I did. She needs your love."

His response is immediate. "She lost my love the minute she cheated on my dad and then chose drugs and alcohol over her family."

"I'm sorry." I don't know what else to say.

"Seeing your mom, your perfect mom was too much."

"My mom isn't perfect, Hunter."

"You know what I mean."

"This whole conversation is total bullshit," I say, sitting up in bed. I am now shouting. "What if I pulled the same shit on you. I mean, *if you ever introduced me to your dad*, I could say the same thing to you. Your dad isn't in prison, is he?"

He's quiet after my outburst. My chest is heaving. I'm furious.

"I don't know what you want me to say," he finally says.

"Call me when you figure it out," I say and hang up.

An hour later he's at my door. I'm still in my pajamas. I haven't even brushed my teeth.

"I thought you had school today?"

"I do," he says. "I'm cutting."

He doesn't look great. And just as I think that, he bows over, holding his stomach and vomits into the bushes by the front door. I draw back in horror.

"Fucking gross," I say.

He looks up at me and wipes his face on his sleeve. "I know."

"Well, come in, so you can wash your face."

He rushes to the bathroom and I hear water running.

When he comes out, there are drops of water on his face and his hair is slicked back.

"I hope it's okay," he says. "I put some toothpaste on my finger to brush my teeth a little."

"I'm still not kissing you," I say.

He gives a weak laugh. "Fair enough."

I pour him a cup of coffee at the bar and he pushes it away. "Sorry."

"You're lucky Oscar's at work so he doesn't have to see your pathetic hungover ass."

He looks down and suddenly I feel bad.

"I'm sorry," I say. "I know it's been a rough few days for both of us."

He nods but still won't meet my eyes.

"When did you start drinking?" I ask.

He squints. "Fourteen?"

"No dork, I mean yesterday."

I expect him to say something like after school, but he says something else.

"Right after I left you guys in Hollywood."

"You're kidding?"

He shakes his head.

"Let's go walk on the beach," I say. "At least that way if you puke again it will be outside."

"Ha ha."

I pull on flip flops and a sweatshirt and we head out.

He seems so dejected that I reach over and hold his hand as we head toward the wet sand near the waves.

"Did your mom have fun?" he asks. I take it as the peace offering it is.

"Yes. She's going to move out here so if you don't like being around her, we should just break up now."

He winces. "Oh God, Kennedy," he says. "It's not like that. It was just hard. Her being here and then seeing my mom…"

"When's the last time you saw your mom, Hunter?"

He stops and looks out at the waves breaking. He speaks without looking at me.

"Two Christmases ago, my dad tracked her down and brought her over for dinner. She was living with some other people at the time. She seemed okay. She was sober for most of the dinner. But, honestly, it was super awkward."

"I'm sorry."

He turns to me. "This is awful and I've never admitted it to anyone, but I was relieved when she went home that night."

I reach for his hand and squeeze it tight. "That's not awful. It's understandable."

He exhales loudly and the puff of air blows his long bangs out of his eyes. "But I guess my dad talks to her at least once a month. He keeps track of her. Even though she doesn't deserve that. It makes me hate him. What kind of douche takes care of someone who fucked him over and fucked his kid over and…" he trails off.

I think about something Oscar once told me. "Did you ever think that maybe he does that not necessarily for her, but for you? And that instead of a weak thing to do, it's actually a strong thing. The easy way out would be to forget she's alive…"

We're back at the house now and he follows me inside before answering.

His face scrunches up. "Huh?"

I shrug. "It's possible."

He tugs on my hand and pulls me to him and soon I'm pressed up against his body.

I push him away. "Go brush your teeth. There's an unwrapped

toothbrush in the medicine cabinet in the bathroom in my room," I say. "I'll meet you in the shower in ten."

We have fast and furious sex. It's weird. It's like we both have pent up anger and frustration. It's hot, but it doesn't feel very intimate or loving. I'm not sure if I love it or hate it.

After, Hunter orders Thai Food to be delivered and then puts on my pink robe to answer the door, which I think is hysterical.

We eat in bed.

"What time is Oscar coming home?" he asks, lifting a long string of pad Thai up to his mouth.

"Late," I say, swirling the last cream cheese wonton in sauce before popping it in my mouth. When I'm done chewing I wipe my mouth and say, "How come?"

"I owe him an apology. And your mom."

I stop eating for a second and he notices.

"What?" he says. "You don't agree."

"I think you should go see your mom."

His eyes narrow. "Maybe if I knew what store she was sleeping behind I would."

"Hunter, I told you that your dad paid for her to go to detox."

"Oh," he says. He shakes his head. "I forgot that. I'm sorry. I started drinking right when I got home that day and only stopped early this morning."

"That's fucked up."

"I know," he says. Then he looks up at me with wide eyes and reaches for his phone. "Did you tell me that on the phone or by text?"

I shake my head. "I don't remember."

He's scrolling through his phone. Then he looks up. "Thank God."

I raise an eyebrow.

"I was making sure I didn't text anything idiotic while I was drinking," he says. "Did I say anything I should regret? Offensive or something?"

I shake my head. "It's fine. Let's just forget the whole thing."

He reaches over and takes my empty plate off my lap, sets it on the nightstand and then climbs above me, hovering, holding himself up on his extended arms so our bodies don't touch. "I have an idea how we can forget about it."

"Sounds good to me," I say, and pull him down onto me.

This time is different than all the others. I don't know if it's because the past few days have been so emotionally charged, but the intensity of the way he kisses every inch of my body is insane.

He lifts my leg and starts to run his mouth up my calf until his lips reach the back of my knee. His mouth travels up my thigh before it wraps around to my front. He kisses every inch of me slowly. So slowly that I'm in agony by the time his mouth reaches mine and I'm moaning and begging him to get on with it.

This time there's nothing but intimacy. He stares in my eyes and my breath is taken away by the intensity of his look.

When he slips inside me I instantly explode in wave after wave of pure pleasure that takes over any conscious thought. It's so intense that I squeeze my eyes shut tightly. I don't know where I am or what I'm doing. I have a vague memory of pulling Hunter's hair and clawing at him and uttering noises I've never heard before.

And when I'm done, my entire body is still on fire.

I open my eyes and Hunter is grinning down at me.

"Whoa."

I'm suddenly shy and turn my head away, but he takes my chin and gently turns it so my eyes meet his.

"That was the most beautiful thing I've ever seen in my life."

7
———————

When Oscar calls and says he's not going to be home until midnight, Hunter and I decide to watch The Dreamers by Bertolucci in the home theater downstairs.

"This is dope," Hunter says, looking around.

"You've been here before, dork."

"I know, but that doesn't mean I still don't think it's cool every time we watch a movie here."

I pause, thinking of his crazy mansion. "I'm surprised you guys don't have a theater. I mean your dad's a director."

Hunter nods. "I think he's so sick of the movies when he gets home he would never use it. I mean he doesn't watch TV or anything."

"Am I ever going to meet the mysterious father of yours?"

"Yes! Soon. I promise."

"I'll believe it when I see it."

I throw open the refrigerator in the corner and ask him if he wants something to drink. The refrigerator has sodas and beers. His eyes flicker over the selection and he grabs a cream soda.

I'm relieved. In the past, he's helped himself to a few beers during movie nights. Maybe he's serious about not drinking so much.

We settle in to watch the movie in leather recliners with blankets on top of us and a big container of popcorn.

The movie is crazy sexy so at one point, we turn off the movie and I climb onto him.

"That's a record," he says when we're done.

"What are you talking about?" I say.

"Three times in one day."

"You're joking, right?" I say. "Hunter West hasn't done it more than three times in one day? Your reputation is greatly exaggerated. Mechanic in the sack, my ass."

He practically spits out his cream soda, sputtering with laughter. "Mechanic in the sack? What the fuck is that?"

"Hunter West, you have quite a reputation in the bedroom and I'm happy to report that you are even better than all the rumors say."

Now he is laughing. "Whoever decided to use a Woody Allen quote to describe my expertise is hilarious."

He squinted. "Are you sure you didn't say that."

I hold up my palm. "Swear."

"Jesus, you girls are worse than the guys."

I plaster a straight face on and say, "You have no idea."

"What makes it so good?" he asks. "You know...the sex?"

"You don't know?"

He shrugs. "Maybe I'm not a typical dude, but I don't talk about this shit with the guys, if you know what I mean. So, in your opinion, what do you think it is?"

"Your size?" I try to be serious but then I burst into laughter. "I'm totally kidding. I have no idea about sizes. You know that. You're my first."

"And only," he interrupts.

I roll my eyes. "But, if I had to say what I think it is, it's that you really seem to care more about me than yourself when we're having sex."

His smile disappears. "But that's just with you, Kennedy," he says.

"You're not like that with every girl you've been with?"

He shrugs. "I mean, yeah, I'm never a selfish dick, but with you, it's different."

He looks away.

"Oh my God, Hunter West, are you embarrassed?"

He looks up at me under his dark lashes and smiles.

"Are you trying to say you like me a lot?" I tease.

He pulls my head close to his so our faces are nearly touching and whispers. "I'm crazy about you. Dead ass crazy."

"Same," I say and kiss him deeply. And then I draw back. "I know what it is!"

He looks confused. "What is?"

"What makes you a mechanic in the sack."

"I'll give you one million dollars if you never use that phrase again."

I ignore him. "It's because when you are making love to me, you make me feel like the most beautiful girl in the world."

He smiles.

"That's it? Well that's easy to do—because you are."

8

The weekend comes and goes without me and Hunter hanging out, which feels a little weird, but he says he's trying to spend the whole time studying to make up for the classes he missed last week.

"I can come over and study with you. Bring you pizza? In a little apron. And nothing else?"

He laughs. "No! You're too much of a distraction."

"I've been called worse."

On Monday morning, he texts and asks if he can pick me up and drive me to school.

When I climb into his car, I inhale. It smells so good. Like Hunter West. My hot boyfriend. He always smells like some delicious cologne he wears and then a big dose of hot pheromones or something, I guess. Whatever it is, it makes him irresistible. I always want to just bury my face in his neck and sniff.

He laughs when I do that now.

"You are crazy, Boots."

I glance down at my boots.

"Yeah, I figured I'd take them out of retirement," I say. "I might have to kick some ass today. That is, if I see Ava."

"Well, they're fucking hot," he says. "Especially when you wear them with those short shorts you have on and that tight top. Jesus, Kennedy, what are you trying to do to me."

He squirms in the driver's seat.

I scoot as far away from him as I can, pressing myself against the Jeep's door. "We have to concentrate on school. Dead serious."

"Then don't wear those boots again," he says.

"No way. I'm not taking them off ever again. They're obviously your Kryptonite, so that means I must wear them every day."

"I thought you burned those. At least you told me that the first day I met you when I said I liked them."

"I lied," I say.

When I first had moved to Pacific High I was the only girl in the school who wore beat-up black boots. And Hunter was nearly the only guy to wear similar ones. He says he knew then we were soulmates. Ha ha.

Shortly after I moved, however, I bought black Vans. All the girls at school wear white ones. It's not that I didn't want to stand out and it wasn't that I cared what Hunter said about my boots, it was more that they're not that practical in a beach town.

But for some reason this morning when I was getting dressed and thinking about Ava and her videotape supposedly proving Josh's attempted rape was consensual and all the idiots at school who might believe her, I unearthed my boots from my closet.

They make me feel strong and powerful. And able to kick ass. If needed.

Not that I would. Ever. Even thinking this makes me cringe. I attacked Hunter's ex once and was mortified. It's taken some therapy for me to believe that I don't take after my physically abusive father.

"Can you meet me after school to film?" he asks.

We're partners in our film class. It's crazy to think we were assigned to the same group with Ava in the beginning of the year. The three of us never actually worked together. Ava dropped the class at the semester break and now it's just me and Hunter.

"Are we totally behind because of the trial?" I ask.

"We've got the first 30 minutes due Friday."

"Guess I know what I'll be doing after school every day this week."

We'd already turned in a short romantic film before winter break. It was awful. We'd gotten a C on it. Pretty shitty for two people obsessed with film. But I'd briefly joined up with two other girls, leaving Hunter in the lurch because Ava wasn't doing shit. I asked to be partnered with him again when we made up, but it was too late: the project was due. We cobbled something together before winter break that was obviously rushed.

Miss Flora wrote me a note saying that she wasn't worried about the "C" grade. She knew we'd both been through a lot that first semester and she'd see our true colors in the new semester.

And now this semester I'm behind because of the stupid trial that was a colossal waste of time and possibly means the entire school things I falsely accused Josh Masters of rape.

I want to cry at Miss Flora's faith in me. I'm not going to let her down. Even if it means missing sleep.

Our current project is a documentary. Well, actually an autobiography. We're supposed to interview each other for it. I have to admit I'm a little nervous. Having Hunter ask about my life, even behind a camera's lens is a little nerve wracking. Not everything is pretty that has happened to me. That's for sure.

"Don't look so bummed," he says. "You get to hang out with me."

"That's the good part."

"What's the bad part?"

I shrug. Luckily, he's just pulled into the school parking lot and we're running late. We jump out and hurry to class, sliding into our seats just as the last bell rings.

The day passes quickly. I'm relieved that I don't see Ava at all. I hang with my friends at lunch. It's great to catch up with them.

Emma says she's done with guys. And that there is no possible way she is going to date any other boy at Pacific High. "I'm waiting for college."

She's going away to some liberal arts school in Iowa. I hate even thinking about her moving. She was my first real friend here.

Coral tells me how she is totally falling for Dex, Hunter's best friend and that how they are both going to UCLA together.

Paige is still dating Greg, a college guy who goes to USC. He's super sweet.

"I think we're getting pretty serious," she says. "He made a reservation at a hotel room down in Laguna for Saturday night." She glances at Emma. "I'm supposedly sleeping over at her house."

"What does your mom and stepdad think about you getting serious?" Coral asks. "Do you think they'll be suspicious?" Paige's mom married Hunter's dad so I perk up.

Paige shrugs. "My mom probably suspects, but my stepdad is always on his movie set."

Hunter's dad is a pretty famous director. Oscar's agent is trying to get Oscar hired as director of photography on a new movie Mr. West is filming this summer. If he does, Oscar is going to hire me as an intern.

"What about when you guys go away to college?" I ask. I partly want to know because it's something I've been thinking about a lot with me and Hunter. But also, because Paige is the brain of our friends and has a full ride to Stanford while her boyfriend is set on playing water polo still for USC.

Paige makes a face. "Yeah. I don't know. What about you and Hunter?"

I nod. "No clue. I've been accepted into both UCLA or USC, but still trying to get into the film schools there. That will be the deciding factor, I guess. I don't really plan to go away since my mom is moving out here. But I told Hunter he should totally go wherever he wants. He got accepted at Emerson in Boston and also the U in Austin."

We all sit there in silence. It's suddenly sobering that this time next year everything will be different. Some of us won't even live here anymore.

The bell rings for class and I'm grateful to leave our now somber table.

After school, I wait for Hunter out at his Jeep. People come and go and still I don't see him. I wonder if I should text him. Then I see something to the side of the school. It's Hunter. He's talking to Ava. He has his back to me so I can't see their hands or read their body language, but it just feels wrong.

My stomach is sour. Before I can react, he's heading my way. I debate whether to tell him off the bat I saw him with Ava or wait. When he gets to me, I decide playing games is bullshit.

"What were you doing with Ava?"

He flushes. It makes my stomach twist again.

"Huh?"

"Don't play dumb, it doesn't suit you. I saw you just now."

"Oh," he says. "Yeah, that was nothing."

"That's all you have to say?"

He meets my eyes now. "Kennedy, you have nothing to worry about. Ava means nothing to me. I've known her for a very long time. Since we were little kids. You can't expect me not to talk to her."

"You're kidding, right?" I say. "After that stunt she pulled in court?"

"It wasn't a friendly conversation just now. You're going to have to trust me on that. I love you. I would never ruin that by even flirting with another girl."

I bite my lip and stare at him. He doesn't look away. One thing I've always believed about Hunter is that he doesn't lie. To a fault.

"Where are we going to film first?" I ask, changing the subject but still feeling sick to my stomach. I'm certain he's telling the truth about not being interested in Ava and not flirting with her, but still there *was* something going on. My body is telling me something isn't right.

"Let's go to the Shake Shack for the first scene," he says. "I'd like to film you answering my questions with your lips on a straw."

"You're a pervert," I say. "But I could use a Date Shake right now so let's go."

When we get there and he sets up the camera while our shakes are being made, I get nervous.

"Why me, first?"

He shrugs. "Dunno. You're prettier?"

"Only reason I'm agreeing to go first is to get it over with."

"Whatever."

Then he's behind the camera and I'm staring into the camera lens.

"What's your earliest memory?" He says, diving right in.

I look off to one side, thinking for a few seconds before I answer.

Then it hits me and I look down.

He lowers the camera. "Kennedy?"

I swallow. "Sorry. This is hard."

He nods. "I know. Remember Miss Flora said nobody but us and her will ever see it, if we want."

"I know."

I take a deep breath. "Okay."

He raises the camera.

"My first memory is of my dad and mom fighting," I say. "I was probably not even in kindergarten yet. Something woke me up. Then I heard them shouting at one another. I got out of bed, bringing my teddy bear with me."

I can see Hunter's smile behind the camera.

"They were in the kitchen."

"Do you remember what they were saying?"

I shake my head. "All I remember is that the bottles that were usually in a cupboard were on the table. Three of them."

"Alcohol?"

"I think so now, but then I didn't know. My dad took a bottle and threw it and it broke on the wall near me. That's when they noticed me."

Hunter lowers the camera and the look in his eyes makes me want to cry.

I look down. He raises the camera again and says, "What happened next?"

"They both ran over to me and were hugging me and crying and saying they were sorry and that what happened would never happen again."

I stop talking. There's a huge lump in my throat. But I take a deep breath and continue. "But it did. Not for a few years, but it did happen again. I didn't think much of it until when I was in high school and my nanna died and dad lost his job. Then it was every night."

"I'm sorry," Hunter says. "Should we take a break?"

I nod. Hunter is tapping his foot and biting his lip. He's really jittery today. I wonder if this is tough for him to do, too. Maybe filming me makes him realize his turn is next. The way he reacted to seeing his mom suddenly has me questioning whether this documentary project is a good idea after all.

Hunter excuses himself and disappears to the bathroom.

I fix my lipstick. I remind myself that going through this is exactly what needs to happen if I'm ever going to make a documentary about someone else. I will totally understand what it's like to be under the spotlight and address difficult memories and topics.

And that has always been an interest of mine. I would love to do a real documentary one day.

Hunter comes back with a carton of French fries and I eagerly dig in.

"Ready to go again?" he says.

"Let's do this."

"What was your childhood like?"

"Besides the occasional blow outs between my mom and dad, it was pretty normal, I think. I had a group of friends in my neighborhood and we would spend our summers running around playing Capture the Flag and Kick the Can and being hooligans until dinner time."

Hunter smiles. "Wow. That's like the kind of childhood you see in movies. It's not like that here in L.A. Not even close. We don't really have real neighborhoods. Jealous."

"Yeah, it was pretty idyllic," I say and smile. "When I was little... before...my dad would always be there to play catch with me or take me to a matinee. He was a more involved dad than most of my friend's dads who were big Wall Street guys. My dad was a firefighter so he was home for days and gone for days."

"Your dad was a firefighter?" Hunter asks. "Cool."

I smile. "Yeah, he was always sort of a hero figure to me."

I swallow. Until.

"Are you still in contact with him?"

I close my eyes. Of course, my mom and dad are the centerpieces of my childhood and I have to talk about them and what happened. I am somewhat surprised that Hunter and I haven't talked much about my dad up until now. I mean, he knows he's in prison. I wonder if he's just asking for the documentary.

"No," I say and look away.

He lowers the camera. "We can edit out anything you're not comfortable with being in the documentary."

"It's fine. Go on."

"Why's that? I mean why aren't you in touch?" he asks.

"He's in prison." I say it and don't fall over dead. It's weird to say it out loud with a camera pointing at me. But in a weird way it feels good, too.

"Are you comfortable talking about that?"

I'm grateful that he asks me this.

"I think so."

"When you're ready."

"My grandmother died around the same time my dad got fired from the fire department for drinking. It started a vicious downward spiral," I say. I pause. I know I sound formal and detached as I describe what happened, reciting clichés. I inhale deeply. "It was the beginning of the end."

"Explain."

"The more he drank, the more violent he got. He never hit me, but he started hitting my mom. And my whole world fell apart," I say. I'd shared most of this with a therapist in the fall. And Hunter knew the basic story, but this felt different, harder. "My mom didn't really try to stop him. I mean she probably did, but it didn't seem like it to me. It seemed like she just put up with it."

"It seems like you might be angry at her for that?"

I look up and blink. I process that for a few seconds. "Yeah. Yeah, I guess I am."

"You want to talk more about that?"

"One day last year, I came home and my dad was beating up my mom. I mean he'd hit her before and then apologized and cried to both of us, but this time was different. This time he didn't stop. He was kicking her while she was on the ground. I had to hit him over the head with a baseball bat to stop him."

The camera instantly drops. Hunter is wide-eyed, his mouth open.

I shrug. "Yeah. There you have it." Inside I'm thinking, *now you know that when I attacked Carly, it was my nature. Not a fluke.*

After his ex-girlfriend Carly hit him at school last year, I lost my mind and attacked her. I was suspended and she went to the hospital to be checked out. Thank God I hadn't seriously injured her, but the fact was I had lost my temper and acted violently. Just like my dad.

I halfway expect Hunter to hate me now that he knows the truth.

"Holy shit, Kennedy," he says and reaches over to grasp my hand. "I'm so sorry."

Even though I'm crying inside, my eyes are bone dry. For someone who has been such a cry baby this school year, I have no tears for this.

"Do you want to take a break?" he asks again.

"No."

I go on to tell him how I called 911. How both my parents were taken to the hospital and the police officer took me to my friend Sherie's house because I had no other family. And how when my dad was checked out and determined to be fine from my attack, he was arrested and transferred to jail.

Then, how Oscar flew out and arrangements were made for me to come live with him in L.A.

"And you know the rest," I say.

"I think that's enough for today," Hunter says and puts the camera down. "That was intense."

"Tell me about it."

"Are you okay telling me all this?" he says. "I mean would it be better telling someone you don't know, you think. Like when you talk to a therapist, it's easier."

I shake my head. "No. I'm really glad it's you."

He smiles.

"Want to go do something else?" he asks.

"I think I should just go home and do homework."

"I'm going to go shoot some hoops and then edit some of this."

"Cool."

When we get to my house, he gets out and holds me. He kisses me long and hard and when we draw back I'm smiling.

"What?"

"That Hunter West Effect is something else."

"More where that comes from."

"Hey, should we do your interview tomorrow. Same place. Same time?"

Something flickers across his face. Then he nods slowly. "Yes, let's plan on that. My turn under the microscope tomorrow. Then on Wednesday we'll do your follow up questions and mine on Thursday."

"That'll work," I say.

9

The next morning, I don't see Hunter until he lopes into first period film class right before the bell rings.

"Just made it," he says in a low voice.

I smile. I like that he actually cares about things like being punctual.

After class, he seems jumpy. He is tapping his foot and his eyes aren't staying on my face as I chitchat with him.

"What's going on?" I finally ask.

"I'll tell you later. Long story."

I frown. But then the warning bell rings and he gives me a quick kiss goodbye and takes off down the hall. I hurry to my next class and wonder what's going on now.

At lunch, he's with his friends, as usual, so I go to lunch with Coral and Paige and Emma.

"Girl, when we gonna double date again?" Coral asks.

"Soon, I hope," I say biting into my fish taco. "Should we plan something Saturday night? Maybe something really like a date. A nice restaurant or something?"

"Oh yeah," Coral says. "That way I can dress up."

"Exactly," I say. Coral and I went shopping a few weeks ago and bought cute dresses and heels. In our day-to-day lives, going to school and hanging at bonfires at the beach, they aren't very practical.

"I'll talk to Hunter tonight."

"I'll ask my dad about a good restaurant," she says. Coral's dad is the owner of a luxury hotel chain in Hollywood. He always knows the hot spots, she says.

"Tell him to make sure the paparazzi get a good look at us," I say.

Paige rolls her eyes.

"What are you and your guy doing?"

"Ahem," she says, pointedly.

I slap my forehead. "Oh yeah, Hotel Smutville."

We all burst into laughter.

"What about you?" I say to Emma. "Wanna come as my third wheel? Or, even better, as my date? I can tell Hunter I'm busy."

She smiles. "Thanks, but we've got a hot date with the new Disney movie and my cousin."

"You are a star," I say. "I wish I had a little cousin so I could go watch Disney movies in Westwood."

The Westwood theater is magical.

"You don't need an excuse," she says.

"I know." I don't tell her that I'm more jealous that she has a cousin. My mom and dad were only kids. I really don't have any other family except them. And Oscar. Even though he's not a blood relative. He's better.

After school, when I get out to the parking lot, Hunter is waiting for me.

"Ready?" I ask.

He does not look thrilled and blows out a puff of hair. "I guess." He shoves his hands in his pockets.

"I'll be gentle," I tease. But I can tell he's a nervous wreck. I reach for his hand. "We don't have to talk about anything you don't want to."

Even though Miss Flora gave us questions to ask, she's really chill so if we don't answer every one, it'll be okay.

Once we're settled in at the Shake Shack, I take out my camera.

"Let's do this!" he says and pounds the table so loudly I jump.

He's been a little weird the past few days. I can't help but think it has to do with seeing his mom again and now here I am bringing it all up again. Big time.

"What is your earliest memory?" I begin.

He bites his lip and then smiles.

"It's at the beach," he says. "My mom took me to the beach every single day when I was little. She would sit and read a book and get a suntan and I would play in the sand building super cool castle sand shit beside her. Then she would take a break from her book and walk down to the water with me and teach me to body surf. Even when I was super little, I could swim. I was a fish. I mean swim as in dog paddle, but I could stay afloat pretty good. One day my mom and I walk down to the water. She holds my hand and we go deeper until we are up to my neck and I'm treading water."

He pauses. I smile. He continues.

"And I feel something brush up against my leg so of course I scream bloody murder. I mean, hell, I know about sharks," he says. "My mom looks really scared at first and she immediately dives under water, which scares the crap out of me. Then she comes up and is smiling. 'It's a dolphin, Hunter. She wants to play.' And sure enough, right beside me a dolphin comes up and looks at me."

"No fucking way," I say, even though I'm not supposed to interject comments like that it bursts out.

"Yes, fucking way," he says. "And it looks at me and then swims off."

I put the camera down. "You win. Best childhood memory ever. I bet nobody in our entire class is going to have a memory as cool as that."

"I don't know," he says, "Julian might have a memory of being raised in the jungle by a black panther of something."

We both burst out laughing. "That's a stretch," I say.

"He's pretty bad ass, though, you gotta admit," he says.

Julian is an amazing trapeze artist and gymnast in our film class.

"True," I say. "Okay. Next question: What was your childhood like?"

He frowns. "It wasn't great. I mean once I started school it seemed like my mom got hooked on drugs. She started hanging out with these other Hollywood women. I'd come home and they'd all be in her walk-in dressing room in fancy clothes drinking and—now I realize—doing drugs."

"Drugs?"

"Like at first popping pills to lose weight."

"Speed?"

He looks down and mumbles. "Yeah."

"How did this affect you?"

He shrugs. "I was invisible. She stopped taking care of me. After a while the other women stopped coming over. And when I got home she was either in bed passed out or locked in her room. I started eating cereal every night for dinner."

"Your dad didn't notice?"

He shakes his head. "He was always gone. Same as now. And the rare times he was home, she would put on this big act, get up, get dressed, and act like it was normal."

His voice is so sad. I put down the camera.

"I'm sorry. That sucks. It sounds like you basically raised yourself."

"When I got to fifth grade, she stopped being there at all when I got home from school. She'd come flying in at seven at night or something before my dad got home."

He pauses.

"Where was she?" I ask.

Through the camera lens I can see his Adam's apple bob and he winces.

He exhales loudly. "I guess she was having an affair with her drug dealer."

I wait.

"And then one day she just didn't come home. My dad freaked out. Then he found out that this had been going on for a long time.

And my mom was hooked on drugs. He put her in detox and she came home. But after a month she was gone again. This happened two more times and then she left for good two years ago."

"I'm sorry."

He stands. "I'm done for now."

I put the camera down. "Sounds good. Let's do my follow up questions tomorrow as planned and we can do more from you on Thursday if we need to."

He doesn't say anything.

I stare at him. He's surprisingly composed and seemingly emotionless considering what he just shared with me.

Standing, I reach for his hand. "You okay?"

He looks away from me. "I don't know."

I don't know how to answer that. "Want to go get dinner?" I'm starving.

"Can't. Playing B ball with the boys."

We drove separately so I guess this means I'm going home by myself.

My feelings are hurt. Which is stupid. I'm not a clingy girlfriend. I want him to spend time with his friends. And I insist on spending time with my friends. We aren't attached at the hip. It just sort of sucks that most of this week our time together has been spent doing homework.

"Hey," I say. "Want to go to a nice restaurant with Coral and Dex on Saturday. A double date?"

He immediately shakes his head. "Nah, I'm not feeling it."

Again, it stings. I don't say anything. It seems like his whole world has been turned upside down by seeing his mom. He's acting different and I don't like it, but I have to be there and support him. Obviously, this is a really tough time for him. I need to be supportive.

And unfortunately, this fucking documentary-slash-biography project isn't helping.

He leans over and gives me a kiss but it only grazes my mouth. "See you in the morning," he says and walks out, leaving me sitting there in the Date Shake place feeling hurt.

10

Hunter doesn't come to class the next morning and I'm worried sick. But I can't text him because Miss Flora is giving a lecture and keeps glancing my way. Immediately after class, I text him.

"Hey."

But he doesn't respond.

I decide he must be asleep. I wait an hour and text him again. "You at school yet? Did you accidentally sleep in?"

Still nothing.

I'm wondering if I should go find him. At lunch, I head into the cafeteria. All his friends, including the twins, Dex and Devin, are sitting in their usual spot, but there's no Hunter.

I'm too embarrassed to ask where he is. I mean I'm his girlfriend. I should know where he is, right?

Coral and Emma are at another spot in the cafeteria. Paige had texted that she was going to lunch with Greg who didn't have classes today.

I grab a grilled cheese sandwich and onion rings and sit with Coral and Emma.

Coral is in the middle of a story.

She looks over at me. "I was just telling Emma how Dex came over after school yesterday and my dad just happened to decide to come home from work early."

"Were you caught naked?" I say, half serious.

"God, no," she says. "But my dad walks in and Dex is sitting there on the couch playing some stupid video game."

"What's wrong with that," I say, taking a bite of onion ring.

"Only that he's also drinking a glass of wine. The wine in a bottle my dad had opened the night before with dinner."

"Oops."

Coral's dad is a wine snob.

"It was a $500-dollar bottle of wine."

"Double oops," I say.

"The night before he had some big shot wine dude over and they'd drank only half the bottle. He was looking forward to having more with my mom last night. She hasn't had a chance to taste it."

"That sucks. Did Dex drink it all?"

"No, but let's just say my dad was not happy. He was kind of a dick about it, too. He asked Dex how the wine was and Dex said it was good. My dad rolled his eyes. I swear my dad is never going to approve of anyone I date. Ever."

I'm thinking that I don't care if my dad approves of anyone I date. Ever.

But then it hits me. "Wait? Dex went to your house right after school?"

"Yeah. Devin had to work. Why?"

"What time did he leave?"

"Not until about eight, why the third degree?"

I blush.

"No reason." Except that Hunter had said he was going to go play B Ball with the twins. Well, he actually said "boys" but that was how he referred to Devin and Dex. He left me at the Date Shake at four. And if Dex was with Coral and Devin was at work, that means he lied to me.

And now, he's not at school. What the fuck?

I'm tempted to skip my afternoon classes and go straight to his house, but I decide it's not worth it. If he is lying to me, it would come out one way or the other. It isn't worth jeopardizing my grades because he's being a fuckwad.

When I get out of school, part of me is half hoping that Hunter will be waiting for me in the parking lot with a sheepish look on his face. But I don't see him anywhere.

I drive straight to his house, starting to get pissed off. We're supposed to film more today. If he wants to skip school, fine, but now he is flaking on me and our film project. Not cool.

His Jeep isn't at his house, either. I text him again. No answer. I drive to the basketball court. He isn't there, either.

I text Paige. "Have you seen your stepbrother around?"

I'm sort of embarrassed to ask her, but I'm starting to feel desperate.

"Nah. What's he done this time?"

"Wish I knew," I write back.

I decide to go home in the farfetched chance that he was waiting there for me, but also because I don't know where else to go or what to do.

It's not like him to be flaky. I'm angry and worried at the same time.

I decide I'd text him one last time. If he doesn't respond, then fuck him. I'll edit the footage I already have of him without follow up questions and he'd have to do the same with what he's filmed of me. The first thirty minutes are due in the morning. But I'm angry. I have more questions I wanted to ask to round it out.

I go home and stay up late editing until I know it's the best I can do without more filming. I hope Miss Flora likes it. It seems to be fine. And it's just a rough draft of our first thirty minutes. But I fall asleep angry. Hunter has not replied to any of my messages or texts.

When I wake in the morning, I immediately reach for my phone. There's nothing from Hunter. Now, I'm more worried than angry. What if he's been in a car crash and is dead? What if they haven't been able to identify him and his family doesn't know? Does anyone in his house even know if he's ever home or not? He lives in a room above the garage and his dad works insane hours. He could be missing and nobody except me would even realize it.

Finally, I resort to something I don't want to do. I text Dex and Devin in a group text. "You guys seen or heard from Hunter? We aren't fighting (as far as I know) but he skipped school yesterday and won't return my texts. And we supposed to meet after school yesterday for a film project we're doing."

I wait and to my relief see the little dots on my phone showing they are writing back.

It's Dex.

"He's alive. I'll have him call you."

"What?"

Then nothing.

Motherfucker.

I stare at my phone. What the hell is going on?

11

When it becomes clear that Hunter isn't calling me immediately I get ready for school and then sit there drinking coffee and checking my phone every few seconds until it's time to leave.

His Jeep is parked in the lot at school and so I'm surprised when I walk into our film class and his seat is empty.

After class, Miss Flora stopped me on the way out. "Is everything okay?" she asks.

I exhale but don't answer and she continues.

"Hunter has several unexcused absences," she says. "The principal asked me about him this morning. And I hope it's okay but I know you two are close and want to make sure everything is okay with him."

Her kinds words make me want to cry but I fight it and shake my head.

"I don't know. I'm sorry."

I rush out before I do cry.

And then as I'm hiding in a bathroom stall wiping my tears away, my phone rings.

"Kennedy?"

"Hunter? What the fuck?" Relief floods me.

"Sorry."

"Where were you? How come you haven't answered my texts? Your Jeep is here."

"Yeah. I got a ride home."

I am confused. Why wouldn't he drive? I can only think of one reason.

"Were you drinking in school."

His silence is my answer.

"Jesus, Hunter."

"Wasn't alcohol."

I don't answer and wait him out.

"Edibles. Way too much. It was an awful idea. I'll never do it again. I'm still fucked up."

My eyes close. Fanfuckingtastic.

"You better get in touch with Miss Flora."

"Fuck," he says. "I will."

He sounds miserable, though. But I don't want to encourage him by being sympathetic.

The bell rings. "I've got to go," I say and hang up. After being worried sick and dying to hear from him, suddenly I have nothing to say.

I know I should go to my next class, even though I'm late, but I just can't concentrate.

Grabbing my backpack, I walk out to the school parking lot and head home.

There I call my mom. I just need to hear a sweet voice.

"Honey?" she says in a concerned voice. "Aren't you supposed to be in school right now?"

"Period cramps," I say.

It's not technically a lie. I's true that I have cramps, but I took ibuprofen this morning and I'm fine.

"How's your class?" I ask.

"I'm almost done," she says. "I can't wait to move out and be with you every day."

"Me, too," I say and feel tears forming in my eyes. I'm not ashamed that right now I really want my mom.

"How's Hunter?"

I close my eyes and try to sound normal. "He's okay," I say. "It was really rough on him seeing his mom."

"I bet," she says. "My heart is breaking for him."

"Yeah."

Later, after our call, I tune out by binge watching Buffy the Vampire Slayer episodes that Oscar has on video tape. I have to play them on an ancient VCR player.

Oscar's been bragging about his obsession with the show since I moved. I always make fun of him, but as soon as I start watching, I'm hooked.

I fall in bed early and sleep ten hours.

When I wake in the morning I realize Hunter never calls or messages again.

I'm so angry I could spit. I vow not to call him all weekend. He can call me.

I start working on the next film project we are going to start in a few weeks—a slapstick comedy. I smile remembering what Hunter said about the project the first day of class—how his was going to be a mash up of Jane Austen and Stepbrothers. Dumb.

But the more I think of him, the angrier I get. I thought our relationship was passed all this stupid game playing bullshit.

I settle in on the back deck in the sun with snacks and a notepad and pen. I realize that I love writing screenplays. Hours fly by and I'm totally in the flow. I only break to eat and drink and then am back in the chair until dark. The next morning, I make a fancy coffee and am at it again.

Oscar asks about what I'm doing and then nods approvingly. "That's my girl."

By Sunday night, I have a solid base for the short film I'm going to make. I'm relieved it's a solo project because clearly, I can't count on Hunter right now. I can't count on him to reach out to me so I certainly can't count on him to finish a school project, either, can I?

12

Hunter is in class Monday when I walk in. He looks awful. And he smells.

"Hey, Boots," he says.

But something between us has been damaged. And he knows it. He looks down right away.

"Want to go to lunch?" he says. My back is to him. Class hasn't started yet. Miss Flora isn't there yet.

"I can't," I say without turning around. "I have to make up for a test I missed Friday when I left school early."

"Oh."

I want to scream at him that I walked out on my classes because of his fucking phone call, but I don't.

"Are we still going to meet after school for follow up interview questions?" he asks.

"That was last fucking Thursday," I say. "It's Monday."

"Uh, I'll take that as a no?"

"I turned mine in."

"Oh," he says again. What the hell does he think? "I probably should work on that tonight."

"Do whatever the hell you want."

"I know you're pissed, Kennedy."

"What tipped you off?"

"Can we talk?"

I shrug.

"I was home all weekend ready to talk to you."

"I've got some catching up to do with school this week. Can we get together after school Friday?"

I sigh. "Fine."

Maybe by then I won't be as angry. Or maybe I'll be even more angry. We'll see.

I WAKE UP FRIDAY HOPEFUL. At school, I see Hunter's Jeep in the parking lot and despite everything, I'm looking forward to seeing him.

My anger is slowly fading. I'm anxious to talk things out today after school.

But when I show up in Miss Flora's class, he isn't in his desk. The bell rings and he still hasn't appeared. Miss Flora has started her lecture when he comes rushing in. He looks like crap. He hasn't shaved and he looks like he slept in his clothes and then tumbled out of bed to class.

He doesn't smile as he walks by and sits behind me. But then again, I don't smile at him.

When class is over, he is instantly at the side of my desk.

"I'll wait for you in the parking lot after school," he says.

"Yeah?"

His face crumples. "Come on, Kennedy. You've got to give me a chance to explain."

"Do I?" I raise an eyebrow.

"Yes," he says and he sounds angry.

"Okay," I say and walk away.

At lunch, I hide in the science room to study.

After school, Hunter is waiting in his Jeep near where I parked my minivan.

He smiles when I walk up and rolls down his window. "You hungry? I'm starved."

"Same," I say.

"Why don't you follow me to my house?" he says.

"That's not a restaurant."

"No kidding," he says. "Just trust me."

"Fine," I say, but I smile.

In his driveway, he waits for me to park and then takes me by the hand to lead me into the main house. Then he tells me to sit at the bar in the kitchen.

I watch as he takes stuff out of the refrigerator and bangs around pots and pans.

"Whoa," I say. "Wait a second? You're making me food?"

He turns and grins and my heart melts. "I figure I owe you one of my famous omelets."

"Seriously?"

"Yep. Want rye or sourdough toast."

"Sourdough," I say. Then I smile. "I love breakfast for dinner!"

He turns. "It's not technically dinner. It's lupper."

"Lupper?" and then I laugh. "Lunch and supper."

Then his face darkens.

"What?"

He shakes his head. "My mom used to call it that."

"I like it," I say.

Before long, he's put a plate with buttered toast and a yummy omelet with bacon, cream cheese and scallions. He's even put a tiny sprig of parsley on the side.

"Wow, West, you have all sorts of tricks up your sleeve, don't you?" I say when I am done.

"Just wait." He stands and does the dishes. I don't offer to help, even though in most circumstances I would. I guess I'm still angry and want him to cater to me a bit longer. Watching him clean I feel the strangest emotions—a mix of overwhelming love and sadness. I'm worried about him.

My stomach roils with anxiety about our "talk" that is coming.

When he's done cleaning, he hangs up the towel and glances at a big clock over the dining room table.

"Everyone's home soon," he says. "Let's go to my room so we can talk privately."

I stand without answering.

We don't speak until we are in his room above the garage. It smells like sweat. He rushes around and throws the clothes all over the floor into one corner, opens his window and lights a candle.

Then he takes my hand and pulls me to the bed where we sit.

"I'm sorry for bailing on you," he says looking me in the eyes and then quickly looking away. "I'm sorry for being totally AWOL in every way that counts lately."

I nod. "If I didn't know you better or trust you so much, I would think you were cheating on me."

"I swear that's not it. I'm just having a hell of time with some things."

I know he means seeing his mother again.

"I know it sucks, Hunter," I say. "I get it. But dealing with things by drinking never works. And probably makes everything worse. I mean if you drink during the week and at school like that, you're not going to pass your classes and you're going to ruin your future."

He hangs his head. "I know."

"I don't want to see you do that to yourself."

He nods.

"It was stupid, I know." He rakes a hand through his hair. "I hate that I'm acting like this."

"Then don't."

He grins. "Right? Simple."

I crawl into his lap. "Is there anything I can do?"

He kisses me long and hard. "Lots of things."

I playfully swat at him. "Besides that," I say.

"Why don't we start with that and I'll think of some other things."

13

I don't hear from Hunter on Saturday.

Despite myself, I'm totally bummed.

Not a text. Not a Snap. Nothing.

I think that he's falling apart and that I should probably get off a sinking ship while I can.

Instead of moping around, I'm going to live my own life. I have to. I can't let him bring me down any more. It's hard enough keeping my head above my own quicksand. It's too much to try to save him at the same time.

I call up Emma.

"Let's go cruise the strip," I say.

"You serious?"

"Hell yeah," I say. "Oscar says I can drive the Hummer."

She bursts into laughter. "I'm in."

"I'll call Coral and Paige."

Miraculously all three of my friends are free and two hours later, we're cruising the Hollywood strip in the Hummer.

We are all dressed to the nines. Like ridiculously so. Coral showed up with a gold lame minidress for me to wear and a tiara.

"You brought a goddamn tiara!" I had said.

"Damn straight," she says. "We each get one."

The other girls have on equally as eye catching dresses as mine and they hang out the windows as we cruise, flirting and laughing with boys in Ferraris and Maserati's and then we zoom away. The whole thing is hysterical since they could leave the Hummer in the dust if they wanted.

At one stoplight near a club, the doorman puts a palm up to stop the girl in front of him begging to get in and walks over to us. He looks like a shorter, less-built version of the Rock. He has a great smile for an old guy.

"Why don't you let the valet park your car and come have some free drinks on me, ladies," he says.

We look at each other and I shrug.

After the valet takes my keys, the doorman escorts us through the red velvet rope where a manager is waiting for us at the door.

"Right this way," he says and leads us inside.

We all exchange looks. Cool.

He leads us to a round table in the center of the room overlooking the dance floor. The crowd parts as he walks and several people either say hi to him or side-eye us. It's a strange feeling to be treated like a fucking rock star.

"Champagne?" he asks once we're seated.

I hesitate. *Um, we are not old enough to drink.*

"It's on the house," he says. "You're my special guests tonight."

I've never had Champagne, but I smile. "Sure. Thanks."

I've checked my phone about ten times since we sat down and finally turn it off.

Hunter obviously is going to be AWOL. Again.

When I left his house last night, it seemed like things were good, back to normal. He told me he'd call. And nothing. And I'm too stubborn to reach out to him first.

Now, I'm going to stop thinking about him and enjoy being with my girls. And drink Champagne and maybe get a good buzz on.

When the manager walks away, Emma leans over. "Think that he's trying to date rape all of us?"

Paige nods. "Right? It's fucking weird."

Corals laughs. "No way. We're good for business. Look. Everyone's staring at us."

"Sure," I say. "All the perverts checking out the teenage girls dressed like hookers."

They all laugh. It is sort of creepy, though, how much attention we are getting.

But also, kind of cool. The pulsing music of the club is seeping into my skin making me feel energized and excited. I'd been to a club once in Manhattan, but something about this L.A. club is different. I mean, it's Hollywood. There's always an expectation in the air that anything and everything could happen in a second. There are movie stars and famous people everywhere. A talent scout or casting director could walk in and change someone's life forever. Of course, everyone knows scenarios like that are rare, but that's the magic of Southern California.

The manager brings us a bottle of Champagne and I'm relieved when he opens it right there in front of us. No chance of anything being slipped into our glasses.

After two glasses each, we are giggling and happy so we head for the dance floor.

While we are dancing, there is a small commotion at the door. Flashbulbs go off right outside and then a small group is escorted in by the manager.

We're just heading back to our table when the manager passes by, leading a group of four guys. I vaguely recognize as some boy band.

As they walk past, they pause before our table to let us exit the dance floor and be seated. It's so surreal with the music and flashing lights. It seems like everything is moving in slow motion. It seems like every one of them takes in every one of us. It's so bizarre. We stare at them. They stare at us. Nobody smiles.

Then we are seated and they pass. The manager seats them at the huge round table next to us. I sit with my back to them. What a strange world I now live in.

Coral leans over and whispers. "Holy shit. That's Sunset Patrol."

Oh. That's who it is, I think. They just got new artist of the year or something. They're pretty good.

We are giggling and making funny TikToks when all of a sudden one of the guys is in front of our table.

"Hey," he says and looks right at me.

"Hey," I say without smiling.

"This is going to sound like a total line but we keep being bombarded with girls who want to sit at our table and we feel like dicks telling them no," he says.

I raise my eyebrow. "Sounds like a serious problem," I say, drily.

He laughs. "I know, right?"

I hide my smile. He keeps talking. "Well, we were thinking you guys should come sit with us."

"Is that so? Why would we want to do that when we have this spacious booth here?"

My girls snicker. I hide my smile again.

"I knew you were going to say that," he says with a big grin. I think, *Damn, he's cute.*

I raise my eyebrow.

"The reason you would want to come with us is because we have something you don't."

I can feel my face slam shut. Drugs? More booze? Money?

But he surprises me. "We have tater tots and onion rings. With, get this, ranch dressing."

I start scooting toward the edge. "Move out of my way," I say, playfully pushing Emma who is laughing. "I'm starved."

He bursts into laughter.

We trail behind him to the table and the four guys pile out and let us in so it's girl boy-girl-boy.

I don't even acknowledge the guys, just scoot the entire platter of food over in front of me and pluck a tater tot off the plate and pop it in my mouth.

They all laugh.

"Kidding," I say and scoot the platter back to the middle. "I can share. A little."

Introductions are made. Dylan is the guy who came over to our table. He is sitting next to the dance floor and I'm right beside him. The other guy's names are a little bit of a blur, maybe because of the Champagne. Something like Jonah and Sam and Carson.

After we all scarf down the food and the manager brings another bottle of Champagne, we are trying to talk over the loud music when one of the other guys, Carson, I think, says, "I don't understand how come girls like you don't have boyfriends."

Coral sits up straighter. "Who says we don't?" she says in a haughty tone.

"Do you?" It's Dylan and he's looking right at me. "Do you have a boyfriend? I mean do all of you have boyfriends?"

I blush at his intensity. But I nod. "We do."

I can't believe that he actually looks disappointed. I smile and shrug. "I'm sure you have lots of girlfriends, anyway. Or at least lots of options to find them."

He shakes his head and without looking at me brings his glass up to his lips and drains it.

"You'd be surprised."

Meanwhile as the others start arguing over how sexist Carson is to say that and how girls can go out on their own even if they have boyfriends, I turn to Dylan and say in a low voice, "I find that hard to believe."

He exhales loudly. "It's hard to meet people."

I smirk.

He sees my face and holds up his palms. "I know, I know. It's totally gross to hear me complain about anything. Poor Dylan. Has to tour the world and fight off screaming fans and can't find a real girl to hang out with."

My smirk vanishes looking into his eyes.

"It's not gross," I say, softly. "It probably is lonely."

He nods. "I don't really meet girls like you very much."

"What are girls like me?" I'm genuinely curious.

"Like I said, real girls. The girls I meet want to meet me because of who I am or because I have money or because maybe I can help their music career, or give them clout or ... yada, yada, yada, blah, blah, blah."

I take a sip of my glass. "That sucks."

While my friends are having a blast laughing and filming everyone on their phones, I sit here having a fairly intense and deep conversation with this famous guy. So weird.

"How serious are you and your boyfriend?"

I frown. "Pretty serious."

"Oh."

I reach over and put my hand on his. "Listen, Dylan, I just met you but I have really good instincts on people and you seem like a really decent guy that any girl would be lucky to date."

He smiles and lifts my hand up and kisses my palm.

"Thank you for that, Kennedy Conner."

I'm as astonished by his kiss as I am by him remembering my full name. I'd only said it to sound snobby.

Everyone at the table hoots and hollers and I jerk my hand away. I can feel my face growing hot.

"Sorry," he says leaning in. "Was that inappropriate?"

I smile. "Maybe a little."

Then two burly looking guys come over. "Time to go gents," one of them says.

Dylan moans. "Already?"

One of his bandmates—Jonah? —protests. "Dude, we were just getting started."

"Sorry," the big guy says. "Williams's orders. Your flight leaves at five a.m. You'll thank me tomorrow."

"Okay, okay," Dylan says. They all are grumbling. We pile out of the booth to let them out. Dylan waits until everyone else has walked away and turns to me.

"Can I Snap you?"

I shrug. "Sure." It's harmless, I think. "It's Kennedy Conner 23."

"Got it."

"Have a nice flight."

He smiles and leans over and kisses my cheek. Then he's gone.

My heart is pounding and I feel incredibly guilty. First, he kissed my palm and then my cheek. They are both somewhat innocent on the surface, but I know the intent behind them. His kiss sent shivers of desire through me both times. It's a good thing I'll never see him again. I love Hunter. I would never do anything to betray him or jeopardize that no matter how angry I am at him right now.

After the guys leave, the sparkle has left. All of us feel it.

Emma yawns and stretches. "I'm sleepy."

Paige nods. "Me, too."

Only Coral is still gyrating to the music.

"We should probably go now," I say. "My buzz has worn off and I'm good to drive now."

We pool all our cash to tip the manager, but he refuses it. Instead, he gives us his card. "Call me next time you're in town. I'll always have a booth for you ladies."

The doorman isn't there anymore when we file out. We take our wad of cash and give it to the valet.

When I look down at my phone to plug it into the charger I see that DylanRoxy snapped me ten minutes ago. I blush. He snapped me seconds after I gave him my name.

I don't respond. Maybe I will. Maybe I won't.

14

I'm in a deep sleep when I wake to someone gently shaking my shoulder.

I blink and see Oscar standing there in silk pajamas.

"Damn, Oscar, those are some fancy PJs," I say, half asleep.

"Hey," he says. "Hunter is here. He kept pounding on the door."

"Here?"

He exhales. "Yes. In the living room. I think he's drunk."

"Oh, my God. I'm sorry," I say and scramble to sit up. "I'll go talk to him and drive him home or something. He can come get his car tomorrow."

"I think he got a ride. His car isn't here."

By now, I'm up, tugging on a sweatshirt over my T-shirt and flannel pajama bottoms.

Oscar hesitates at the door to my room.

"Do you want me to come down with you?"

I shake my head. "No, but thank you. I'm sorry."

"You don't have to apologize."

"He woke you up and everything."

"It's totally fine, sweetie."

"Thanks," I say with a grim smile.

Downstairs, Hunter is pacing the area between the kitchen and great room raking his hand through his hair. His eyes are bloodshot and he has on shorts and bare feet.

"Did you forget your shoes?"

"Jesus, Kennedy are you trying to kill me?" he says, shouting.

I back up, eyes wide. He knows that I will break up with him in a second if he yells at me or loses his temper. We've had this conversation. He knows that my dad's temper has made my own tolerance for guys with anger a big fat zero.

He sees the look on my face and closes his eyes. "God, I'm sorry. I'm dying over here." This time he says it in a normal voice

"Well, I'm sure being drunk doesn't help whatever is upsetting you."

He thrusts his phone out at me. "This."

I blink. "What?"

"This."

It's a TikTok. I look at the username. Sunset Patrol. My heart sinks.

"It's not what you think."

"Just watch it and then tell me what you think I think," he says in a nasty tone.

I hit play.

It's Dylan kissing my palm and then it cuts to him kissing my cheek.

The words on the TikTok say, "When you meet the girl of your dreams but have to catch an early morning flight."

"I had no idea someone was filming," I say without thinking.

I'm slightly horrified, but also flattered. Because its TikTok it plays on repeat. I wince. I'm sure it is horrible for Hunter to see.

Hunter draws back, eyes wide as if I've punched him. "That's all you have to say about it?"

I reach for his hand. "No. It's nothing. I swear," I say. He jerks his hand out of mine.

He backs away from me.

"Hunter, you're drunk so I'd rather talk about this tomorrow, but I swear what you see is what you get." Again, wrong thing to say.

"Jesus fucking Christ, what are you trying to say, Kennedy?" He sounds so hurt my heart is breaking.

I exhale loudly. "We sat with this band. That's it. We told all of them we had boyfriends right off the bat. It was purely platonic."

He closes his eyes as if he's using the last shred of patience. Then his eyes fly open. "Why is he fucking kissing you, then?"

I frown. "I don't know. I told him it was inappropriate. He's just sort of an affectionate person. Honestly, Hunter it means nothing. I swear. I'm never going to see him again."

He sees my phone clutched in my hand at my side and looks at it pointedly.

"He's just sort of an affectionate person?" he repeats. "You fucking know him that well?"

I wince again. "Hunter—" I begin, but don't know what to say.

"So, you didn't arrange to stay in touch? Like you don't have his phone number or Snap?"

I can feel my face grow hot.

"It was his idea."

"Of course, it was." He strides by me angrily toward the front door.

"Hunter?"

"I'm outta here."

"You're drunk."

"No shit." I flinch at his nasty tone. It's like he hates me suddenly. Maybe he does.

The front door slams. I follow him and open the door. He's slumped on the front porch with his head between his hands.

I sit down beside him in the dark so our knees are touching. He doesn't move away.

"I thought you weren't going to drink like this again?"

He doesn't answer, just shakes his head.

"I thought you weren't going to kiss strange boys again."

"Come on. You saw everything. That was it. Obviously, I wasn't kissing him."

He doesn't look up. "I know. I just can't stand the thought of someone else spending time with you, sitting and laughing with you, falling in love with you."

"You were my first choice tonight, Hunter, but you didn't call." The words aren't exactly right. It makes it sound like I chose Dylan as second choice and that's not right, either.

"I know. It's all my fault."

I reach for his hand. "Hunter, I'm worried about you."

He pulls his hand away. "You don't need to worry. I know what I'm doing."

"Well, listen, I can drive you home. Let's go," I reach for him again.

He tips over and slowly lays back with his head on the pavement behind us.

Oh great.

Oscar is suddenly there. He reaches down and grabs Hunter under the arms from behind and hoists him up. "Come on, buddy. You're having a little sleepover."

Hunter mumbles something and then leans over and pukes on the cement porch.

While I wash it down, Oscar carries Hunter into the guest room on the first floor.

I help him get Hunter under the covers. Oscar gets an old plastic ice cream bucket and puts it on the nightstand. "Hope he doesn't choke on his vomit."

I look up, horrified.

Oscar sighs. "I can stay up and watch him."

I shake my head. "No, I'll sleep in here and make sure he doesn't."

"Holler if you need anything."

Oscar leaves, closing the door behind him.

15

I grab a throw blanket and lay on top of the covers near Hunter because it would feel awkward to crawl under the covers with him when Oscar knows I'm down here in bed with my boyfriend. Plus, I want to be able to jump up if Hunter needs my help.

I don't sleep well at all. Hunter does sit up once and I rush over and put the ice cream container under him as he pukes. By the time, I get back from flushing it down the toilet and rinsing out the container, he's back asleep again. I stand over him holding a warm washcloth I'd brought to wipe his face, but decide it's not worth waking him. I'll wash all the sheets in the morning.

When the sun pours into the room filtering through the curtains, I haven't slept barely at all. Meanwhile, Hunter is snoring loudly.

I'm tired, have a headache and I'm cranky when I plod into the kitchen to start some coffee.

By the time the coffee is brewed, Oscar is up, showered and dressed for a day on the set.

He looks at me and without a word, walks over and gives me a big hug. It's exactly what I need.

When he pulls back, he says, "I can call in to the set if you need me?"

I shake my head. "I'm good."

He nods. "Call me if you need anything. I'm serious."

Hunter sleeps another three hours. After some coffee, I end up crawling back in bed with him, but of course because of the coffee I can't sleep. I do doze off a little. I wonder if last night is what it feels like to be the mother of a newborn – sleeping but not sleeping, alert for any danger or need.

I babysat a three-month-old once and that was one of the hardest nights of my life. The baby cried the entire four hours despite what I did. It was terrifying.

The mom paid me extra, I think, because she felt so bad.

Finally, later, Hunter rolls over and opens one eye to squint at me.

I don't smile. Just stare.

He moans and then yanks the covers over his head. I slap at the blankets. "Get up! My turn to sleep."

It's true, I'm just starting to feel like I can actually fall asleep again.

"You didn't sleep?" he says, sitting up.

I yawn. "Not really. I was up all night worried you were going to choke on your puke."

He winces. I'm glad.

He puts his face in his hands. "I'm sorry." The words come out between his fingers.

"Let's talk later," I say. "I seriously am dizzy from lack of sleep. You can help yourself to a shower and food. Wake me in a few hours and we can talk and I'll drive you home."

I turn my back to him and pull the covers over my head.

The light has changed when I poke my head out again so I'm sure I've slept, but I don't really feel like it. I feel heavy, sluggish.

I stumble into the living room. Hunter's not there. There's a note on the bar. "I wanted to let you sleep. I got a ride home."

For some reason, it pisses me off. I know he thinks he's being thoughtful, but to me it feels as if he didn't want to talk to me or see me.

After washing the sheets, showering, and putting a clean pair of pajamas back on, I settle in at the bar counter to do homework. The doorbell rings. My first thought is Hunter is back, but when I look, it's a delivery guy with flowers.

I don't hide the disappointed look when I fling open the door and grab the flowers. Pink roses.

I throw them on the counter and rip open the card.

"Can you forgive me?"

I text him. "I'm staying home tomorrow to work on our film project. Be at my house tomorrow at six so we can brainstorm the second half. We can talk after."

"Okay. But it's not due until Friday."

"I'm using it for my college submission. For me, it's due at eight in the morning on Tuesday. I need you to help me edit the second half. Remember, it's going to be a montage based on my interview with you. I want to make sure I get it right."

He's quiet for a few minutes. I close my eyes. I was worried about this.

"Did you change your mind about letting me use your interview for the submission?"

He's silent for a few seconds. "Kennedy? I don't know. I didn't realize."

I swallow. He's right. It was maybe too personal.

"Let me know," I say. "Tell me by tomorrow morning since I'm not going to school, I can scramble to put something else together, okay?"

"Okay."

I hang up and want to break something. Fuck. I need to pass my film class. I'm applying for the USC and UCLA film schools and obviously, I need to have a good body of work to show. I was waiting to send the application until we finished this one project.

I email Miss Flora Monday morning and tell her I'm going to be absent because I have to scramble to do a film for my film school applications. She sends back a smiley face and says, Good Luck and asks when my submission is due. When I tell her its due at 8 a.m. tomorrow, she writes back.

"I'd love to write you a recommendation letter. I'll get it to you today. Maybe late because I have some stuff after school, but I will get it to you before the deadline tomorrow morning."

I am thrilled, but also embarrassed. The college requires a letter of recommendation and I have been so wrapped up in drama with Hunter, I forgot. Miss Flora is saving me.

I spend the day working on editing of the footage.

I don't hear from Hunter so I figure we are good to use the interview. When he gets here, we can order a pizza and work until late.

Six o'clock comes and goes. By eight, I am spitting mad, as Oscar would say.

I text Hunter. "What the fuck?"

There is no response.

Hunter never calls.

I vow not to let my relationship with Hunter West ruin my future and career.

Then at ten, I'm crying with frustration and feeling helpless. I will need to do a new project without his stuff. It will take me all night.

Oscar comes home at 10:30 and I beg him to let me interview him.

I film him and it includes the story about him getting kicked out of the house.

It's pretty emotional. At points, we are both crying.

At two in the morning, I check email and Miss Flora has the letter for me. It makes me cry again.

I work all night. It's due at 8 a.m. and hit submit at 7:30 a.m. After I hit send, I double check the confirmation email and crawl into bed.

I sleep most of the day. I never hear from Hunter.

16

When I return to school the next day, Wednesday, I head straight to film class. I'm early, but Miss Flora is already there.

"Thank you so much for the letter," I say. "I think I got my submissions in on time. I totally dropped the ball on asking for the letter. Thank God you remembered and then offered."

She smiles and then frowns. "It's none of my business, but I'm worried about your project with Hunter."

"I am too." I say. "Can I submit the project solo? I mean is that allowed?"

She purses her lips together and then nods. "I think in this case we can make an exception. And it should be fine to do on your own. And then you don't have to worry because the final project is actually a solo project, but you can do both that way."

"Thanks." I don't tell her I've already written a script for the slapstick.

At lunch, I meet the girls and we go off campus to the taco stand overlooking the beach.

"Girl!" Coral says. "We've missed you."

Paige looks right at me. "I'm gonna guess it all has to do with Hunter?"

I nod. I feel tears prick at my eyes.

"I'm sorry he's acting like this," Emma says. I look over at her. I've pretty much kept most of it to myself but, apparently, all my friends know.

Paige explains. "He came home drunk and his Dad went ballistic."

"What night?"

I try not to ask.

"Last night."

I guess he'd gotten away with it for a while.

"They had a blow out and Hunter took off. He never came home. Was he at your house?"

"Nope. Not last night."

"His Jeep is still there, so I don't know. I thought maybe you'd come to get him."

I shake my head. And suddenly I'm filled with jealousy. It could be Dex or Devin or any other guy friend who got him, so I'm not sure where the feeling stems from. What I do know is that my once reliable boyfriend is no longer reliable and probably not even my boyfriend anymore.

Hunter calls me right when the bell rings at the end of the school day. He must've been waiting.

"Hey," I say, wary.

His voice sounds hoarse. "I fucked up," he says.

"Yeah."

"Even more than flaking on you."

My heart is racing and I can feel it in my throat. "What happened?"

"I know I said I wasn't going to drink ..." he leaves it at that.

It takes me a minute to compute. "Wait? You were on a bender?"

He grunts. "Worse."

"My God. Where were you?"

"I don't want to tell you. But I never want to lie to you."

Now, my heart sinks. I close my eyes. "Better get it over with."

He clears his throat and I hold my breath. I have no idea what he's going to say. No fucking idea. But I know it's going to be bad.

And it is.

"I was with Ava."

I feel my knees grow weak.

He speaks quickly. "But it's not like what you think. We're just friends. It's just that she was the only way I could get ..."

"Get what, Hunter?"

"She has a ... dealer."

Now I'm about to puke. I clutch my stomach trying to wrap my head around what he just said.

"You were doing drugs." And here I thought he was just drinking.

"I'm sorry." He whispers the words. "I just didn't want you to worry anymore and I promised you I'd never lie to you."

And then he hangs up.

I rush out of school blinded by my tears.

I'm not crying because I'm sad. My tears are from anger and frustration.

The boy I love is going off the fucking deep end and I don't think there is anything I can do to stop him.

17

At home I tug on my running shoes and hit the beach. An hour later I come back home and feel less like murder.

I have to tell someone and don't want to tell my girls yet because they will judge him and God knows whether Paige will tell his dad. So, I tell Oscar.

I pace our deck overlooking the beach in my flannel pajama pants and a sweatshirt until Oscar walks in at eleven. I'm usually in my room getting ready for bed at that hour so he jumps when I fling open the French door.

"¡*Dios Mío*! Kennedy, you scared the crap out of me!"

"Sorry."

He takes in my face and immediately says, "What's wrong?"

I fight back tears that have formed upon hearing his sympathetic tone.

"It's Hunter. Now I think he's doing drugs. Well, I don't think, I know—he told me he did them. And he did with Ava. And he keeps missing school. I'm just so worried." I blurt it all out in a rush.

He pulls out a bar stool at the bar counter and pats it with his hand.

"Sit here. I'm gonna make you some hot chocolate. That's what your grandmother did for me when I was upset about something."

"She did?" I still can't imagine my cranky grandmother as the motherly person she apparently was to Oscar and my mom.

He's at the stove heating up milk and dumping in cocoa when he says. "Yeah. And she made homemade whipped cream for on top, but you're going to have to settle for the stuff in the plastic container."

"I'll take it."

We decide to skip the bar stools and go out on the deck since it is such a beautiful night with a big nearly full moon over the sparkling waves. Once we are settled on the back deck—in lounge chairs under piles of blankets, holding warm cups of cocoa and staring out at the water—I tell him more. It helps that my face is in the near dark.

"I don't know what to do," I say. "I want to tell his dad, but I don't think he'll ever forgive me if I do."

"Hmm," Oscar says. "That's tricky."

"I think I should give him a chance to quit on his own."

"You think he will?"

"I don't know."

"Aren't you guys doing a school project together?" Oscar asks.

"I got out of working with him because he kept flaking."

"That's not cool," Oscar says.

I wince. One thing I don't want to happen is to have Oscar not like Hunter. That's my only hesitation in having this conversation.

I get up. "Thanks, Oscar."

"Of course."

Oscar didn't really give me any solutions, but he did listen. And that means a lot.

Once I'm in bed I wonder if I could have had the same conversation with my own dad. If things had gone differently if he would be that kind of dad. Sadly, I don't think so.

18

Hunter isn't in school again.

But he texts me. "Can we talk after school?"

I don't answer.

When I pull in my driveway that afternoon, he's standing there by his Jeep waiting.

"I guess you can come in," I say.

We sit on the couch. It feels awfully formal, but whatever. I'm still angry.

He throws his head back and exhales and then speaks staring at the ceiling.

"I don't know what to say except I'm sorry and can you forgive me?"

Then he dips his head and looks at me.

"Hunter, it's more than that. You not only flaked on me—for something important—our school project and the deadline for my film school app, but then you were doing drugs and were with Ava," I say. "I mean one of those things alone sucks, but all three?"

I just shake my head.

"I know it sounds like a lame excuse, but I didn't want any of that to happen–the drugs or Ava or flaking on you. It just worked out that way."

I stop myself from rolling my eyes or telling him to take some fucking responsibility for his actions. He keeps talking.

"I was really in a bad place and I was drunk. I just wanted something to make me feel better."

"Was that the first time? And what did you do?"

He shakes his head. "Took some OxyContin. Last year I tried it with Ava. Her dealer actually lives a few houses down from my place. I knew I couldn't drive drunk," he looks at me. "I'm not that idiotic. Instead, I walked over to the guy's house and he let me in and I bought some. He told me I could just chill there. He was having some friends over. I didn't really want to stay, but I also didn't want to deal with my dad, either."

I don't say anything. He keeps talking.

"We were just chilling watching Fantasia when people started coming over."

"Fantasia?"

He looks at me. "That's what I love about you, you're so innocent."

I scowl. "Keep going."

"A few people came over and then Ava walked in."

He pauses and looks at me. I keep my face expressionless.

"She comes over to me and says she's sorry about everything. That Josh basically made her testify. That he has something—she won't tell me what—that he's holding over her head. She said she had no choice."

"Sure," I say, my voice filled with skepticism.

"I know she's awful, but I actually believe her."

I roll my eyes, but don't say anything.

"Oh!" he says suddenly. "I forgot an important part. She was with her new boyfriend."

"Why's that important?" I say, playing dumb.

He blushes. "So, you know it wasn't anything funny going on."

"You told me to believe you and I do," I say and I mean it.

He exhales. "Thanks," he says it in a low voice.

I stand, ready for him to leave. I think I've heard enough for one night.

"What?"

"Hunter, there's so much more. I mean, you haven't even addressed why you were doing drugs? I mean I thought that was taboo for you. I didn't know you'd already experimented with Ava."

"I don't have an excuse," he says in a low voice. He's sitting on the edge of the couch, his head hangs down and he's not looking at me. "The only thing I can say is that seeing my mom really has fucked me up."

"I get it," I say. "But there's got to be a better way to deal with that." He shrugs.

"I'll help you, Hunter. If you need my help, I'll help. I can drive you to therapy appointments or whatever. I want to help you."

For a second I think he's going to start crying but then he stands and gives me a sad smile.

"The best thing you can do is just love me. I'm fucked up, Kennedy. I know I don't deserve you."

I stare at him and wonder if I have the guts to say what I'm going to next.

Finally, I do.

"I do love you, Hunter. I really do. But I can't be with you if you are going to do drugs and flake on me. I just can't. I can't have a guy in my life who I can't count on. I'm sure you understand that."

He swallows and nods. "I'll do better."

"Maybe you should go now," I say. "I'm exhausted."

And as I say it, I realize I am. Emotionally and physically and mentally exhausted from this whole week.

"Can I pick you up tomorrow? We can grab a bite at this really killer restaurant right on the beach. And then maybe just sit and watch the sunset?"

"Maybe," I say.

I want to ask him what he has planned for the rest of the night since it's still pretty early, but I stop myself. I refuse to be that kind of girlfriend. I'm not going to monitor his every move. I'm not going to be suspicious. I'm going to let him do his thing. And if his 'thing" involves me and being a good boyfriend, then we're going to work out just fine.

If it means doing drugs? Then I'm out.

In my driveway, he reaches for me and draws me in for a hug and then kisses my brow.

"I'll be here right at six."

After he climbs in the Jeep, he rolls down the window.

"Kennedy, I never want to do anything to hurt you."

I nod.

But I also know that just because he doesn't want to doesn't mean he won't.

19

The next day I yank out a dress I've been saving. It's a sundress that buttons up the front. It's black with tiny red roses. I fell in love with it in the store. I'm especially careful with my makeup and suddenly excited to go to a nice restaurant.

But then six comes and goes.

At seven, I text him two words. "Fuck you. We're done. I'm out."

I'm devastated but also relieved. I should've done this a long time ago.

I try to escape into a movie on the couch. I curl up with a blanket and am watching Jane the Virgin when I must fall asleep because the sound of someone pounding on the front door wakes me.

I look at my phone to see what time it is—1 a.m.—and see ten missed calls and just as many texts. Hunter. I guess I know who's at the door. I push the door open and turn and walk away. He hurries inside.

"I know. I blew it. I was over at Craig's house and he offered me some beer and one thing led to another. And then I had to wait until I was okay to drive. And I came straight here. Can you give me another chance?"

I look at him. He looks awful. I don't even know who Craig is.

That's how far apart we've become. There are so many things I could say. But instead, I shake my head.

"I need some time, Hunter."

"How long?"

"I don't know," I say honestly. "I told you I can't be with someone I can't count on."

"I know that." His voice is quiet. But his eyes are wild. "I'm such a fuck up." He mumbles it under his breath. I don't have the energy to feel bad for him. I'm over it.

"Just go, Hunter," I say.

I love him. But I love sober Hunter. Drunk Hunter is a whole different story.

"I think you're being unreasonable," he says.

That word sets something off in me. It's like a match has struck a flame and I honestly see white and then red and before I know it, I've picked up something—I don't even know what because I can't see straight—and chuck it across the room where it breaks into shards and then I take my arm and sweep it across the counter filled with plates and glasses and the sound of glass breaking finally sinks in. I stop, frozen.

I don't know where I went just then. I'm horrified to realize I just lost my shit. My anger sent me into a dark black hole. Out of control. And when I look at Hunter, he just stares at me and backs out of the door.

I turn my back to him. My chest is heaving with fury and my hands are clenched into fists.

I don't even turn around until I hear the door click behind me. I creep to the front window and peer out where he can't see me. I see him by his Jeep. He's kicking the tires. Then he punches the side of the car. I see red blossom on his knuckles.

Again, I want to feel sorry for him. But I don't. Instead I'm still overwhelmed with a white-hot fury.

I sink to my knees and cry. I *am* my dad. I have the same anger and violence inside me. I've just proven it. Crying, I pick up the pieces of glass. It takes me thirty minutes but I manage to clean up my mess and only cut my hand twice.

I leave Oscar a note. As I write it, a tear drops onto the center of the paper and I have to start again.

"I'm sorry I broke a few plates. And a glass. And that vase that the flowers came in last week. I don't have an explanation. I'll pay for everything. Please forgive me."

Even though my mind is racing with so many awful thoughts, I crawl into bed and fall asleep right away.

In the morning, Oscar has replied to the note. "It's all good. Let me know if you need to talk."

I feel instantly guilty.

Hunter isn't in film class. Of course, I'm worried so I text Paige.

"Did he ever come home? He wasn't in class."

"He came home this morning. But I think his dad took him to rehab."

"What?"

"I left for school while they were still arguing about it, but that was the plan."

20

The rest of the week I concentrate on school. I go to class, come home, study and do my homework. I sleep ten or eleven hours a night. I know this is not normal. I feel like I'm in survival mode. I try not to think about Hunter in detox. He's not my problem anymore. But deep down inside I miss him and my heart is breaking.

My girls are busy all week too so they don't really see how I'm falling apart. They shoot me a few concerned texts, but I tell them I don't want to talk about it. But when Friday rolls around, a group text goes around.

"Let's go to Magic Mountain tomorrow," Emma writes.

"Sounds like a drug trip," I write, trying to be funny, even though I still feel like screaming and crying. I need the distraction.

"HA!" Coral writes. "It's an amusement park. Roller coasters, cute boys, etc."

That's what I thought. That's what I was afraid of. But I think it's a sweet attempt on their part to cheer me up.

"I don't do roller coasters," I write back. I remember Hunter trying to get me on one at the pier.

"Wimp," Paige writes. "J/K." Just kidding.

"I know," I write.

"Lots of other rides and stuff. You in?"

"Why not. No peer pressure on the roller coaster though."

"Deal."

AFTER SCHOOL, Oscar texts me. "Hey you got plans tonight?"

"No. But tomorrow night I'm going to Magic Mountain. Wish me luck. I'm deathly afraid of roller coasters."

"Can't help you. I quit coasters at age 30. They make me barfy."

"Same. At least I imagine same. I'm stealing your excuse."

"Help yourself. The excuse is all yours. Want to hang out tonight?"

He knows I broke up with Hunter. I think he's worried about me. It's sweet.

"Yes."

"Good! I've got a surprise. It's a party. With celebs. No cut-off jeans. Ha."

"In case the paparazzi catch wind that I'm there and show up to take my picture?"

"Eeexaaactly. Be ready at eight."

My friends had bought me a red body hugging dress with a sweetheart neckline that I like but that makes me feel like a neon sign. I try that on and then rip it off. Nope.

Then I go through every dress I own and discard them all. What do you wear to a party with celebrities? No fucking clue. Finally, I pick up a simple black dress. It has a square neckline and is sleeveless with thick straps. It hugs my curves but also is not revealing. There's no cleavage and it is long—for me—and goes to just above my knee.

I figure that since all the celebrities there are going to be wearing the revealing dresses and high heels so I'll show up the opposite. I also slip on some cute sandals that aren't super high.

I put on some dangling green earrings that match my eye color and figure it's the best I'm gonna do.

When Oscar sees me he lets out a low whistle that makes me blush.

"You are stunning my dear."

"Oh, stop."

"It's true. Every woman at the party is going to be jealous."

I frown. That was not the goal.

"Don't worry. They will also love you to pieces. I mean, my God, who wouldn't?"

I smile. Oscar has been really good for my self-esteem since I've lived with him. Gay men have a way of making straight women feel beautiful no matter what.

Despite that, as soon as we walk into the party, on the rooftop of some fancy L.A. hotel, I feel like a hick and a little kid playing dress up.

All the women have skintight dresses that leave nothing to the imagination. There are legs and cleavage everywhere. No heel is under four inches. There isn't a woman at the party that I can see who doesn't have hair and makeup that wouldn't work on a runway or magazine cover.

A lot of people come up to us and hug Oscar. Everyone loves him. Of course. He introduces me and everyone is nice, although the women give me the up and down and then dismiss me.

After a while, Oscar turns to me. "Want a soda or something."

"Sure."

"Go grab that spot by the rail and I'll grab us something to eat, too."

I'm not hungry but I smile my thanks. He leaves and I see what spot he's talking about. There's a group of chairs with cushions. I make a beeline for it. I'm not comfortable meeting a ton of people at once. I'd rather sit in the corner and people watch.

I settle in and can finally take in the party in a less overwhelming way. There have to be at least three hundred people crowded onto this rooftop. Most are gathered under the heat lamps and near the bar.

From my new vantage point, I start to pick out the famous faces I recognize: It girls. Movie stars. Models. Athletes.

It would be awkward and geeky to take out my cell phone and record, but I'm super tempted to do so. My new California friends would think I was a dork for being star struck since they've been raised around celebs their whole lives, but Sherie back home in Brooklyn would squeal with me.

Oscar is back with drinks and a plate of cheese and crackers and other finger foods I don't recognize.

He smiles at me as I eat and drink.

"How you doing, kiddo?"

"Good," I say and smile back. I'm lying. I'm not doing awful, but I sure have been better. I miss Hunter and I'm mourning our relationship. Some part of me takes comfort in doing it now instead of in the fall when we might both go off to separate colleges, but it still hurts.

And thinking that, I realize that I might be the only one going off to college. He's probably missed so much school he might not even graduate. Way to zero in on the bad boy bully flunk out, Kennedy.

A group comes over and starts talking excitedly to Oscar about something that happened years ago. Some crazy story about Oscar saving the day when some diva actress went off the rails and demanded all these crazy things before she would come out of her trailer to film. Oscar somehow had her in tears and apologizing to everyone before the day was over.

"So, what exactly did you say to her, Oscar?" One woman in a white and silver mini dress says.

"A gentleman never tells," he says.

They all laugh.

"Oh, look!" another woman says. "Maxwell Hughes just showed up. We better go kiss his ass."

Oscar stands. "Want to meet him?"

I shake my head with my eyes wide. I've heard about his reputation as a tyrant.

Oscar laughs. "Okay. I'll be right back."

Hughes is a big shot studio head. I glance through the crowd to see what he looks like but don't see anything.

I stand and turn, facing the edge of the roof. The downtown L.A. skyline is no New York, but it's not bad.

"Penny for your thoughts?" a voice says at my elbow. I jump. It's Dylan.

I can feel my face grow warm. I smile and turn back to the view.

"If I tell you, you'll think I'm being a bitch."

"Oh, good, now I really want to know. I bet you're thinking that all these women spent all this money on their outfits and hair and that you look a million times better than any of them and I bet you just threw on the first thing you found."

I whirl on him with my mouth wide. "What? That might be the most passive-aggressive, backhanded compliment and insult I've ever received in my entire life. I look like I just threw on the first thing I found?"

My voice is teasing, but he blanches and closes his eyes. "Jesus, did that come out wrong."

"I'll say. And it wasn't the first thing I found. I decided on this dress after trying on every single thing in my closet and deciding that nothing looked good so I might as well just settle on something that was comfortable."

He laughs. "I'm going to try again, keeping it simple this time," he says. He lowers his voice and meets my eyes and I feel a chill run across my scalp and find it impossible to look away from his dark brown eyes. "You look stunning. Period. That is all. End of story."

"Thanks."

"You still haven't told me what you were thinking about that would make you seem like a bitch?"

"Oh that," I say and toss my hair over my shoulder. "I was thinking that even though it's not New York, the L.A. skyline isn't half bad."

"Half bad?" he says and then nods. "You're right. We do try. Hey, are you from New York?"

"Yes."

"Why don't you have a New York accent?"

I shrug. "I don't know."

"Oh."

"I thought you were on tour?" I say. He'd snapped me a picture of him near the Eiffel Tower last week and I had forgotten to Snap him back with all the Hunter drama going on.

"If you hadn't left me on red, you would've known that I was back in town," he says. "Tours don't last all my life, you know."

I laugh. "Actually, I don't know." I feel bad for leaving him on red, but I didn't want to lead him on by opening his Snap.

"Well, they don't."

"Okay, now I know."

"Big brain on Kennedy."

"Just wait."

I like bantering with him. The conversation with him is light and easy and fun. It feels good. All my conversations and interactions with Hunter l are always so fucking deep. At least lately.

But then Dylan has to go get all intense on me too. What's up with California guys?

His smile fades and he stares at me, his eyes going down to my mouth. "I like that you are such a mystery to me, Kennedy Conner."

I look away.

He sighs. "I know. You have a boyfriend. Yada yada yada. Story of my life. Every girl I like is already taken. Blah. Blah. Blah. Boring story."

"Every girl you like? I guess I'm on the list of girls you like, then?"

He leans over his phone and types something.

He makes a face and types some more.

"God, this is so hard," he says.

"What?" I say.

"Making a list of all the girls I like."

"Oh, brother," I say, teasing. "I suppose we'll be here all night while you type. It probably says your favorite words: blah, blah, blah, yada, yada, yada."

Dylan snickers but keeps his head down typing.

I see Oscar heading our way and then he stops, sees me talking to Dylan and beelines in another direction. Crap.

Dylan thrust his phone at me. "Will you look at my list and make sure it's okay, you know, up to your high standards?"

"Fine!" I say and give a pretend huff.

I take his phone and look down.

Kennedy Conner

Kennedy Conner

Kennedy Conner

Kennedy Conner

Kennedy Conner

Kennedy Conner

Kennedy Conner

Kennedy Conner

Kennedy Conner

Kennedy Conner

Kennedy Conner

Kennedy Conner

Kennedy Conner

Kennedy Conner

Kennedy Conner

Kennedy Conner

Kennedy Conner

It goes on for as long as I can scroll. I hand it back to him.

"So, what do you think?" he says. "Anyone I should cut?"

"It's, uh, interesting."

I glance up and see Oscar smiling at me. Dylan looks over and frowns.

"Wait? Is that guy your boyfriend?"

I'm taking a drink of my soda and I practically spit it out. "What?"

He shrugs.

"That's gross. He's old enough to be my dad. He's practically my uncle. He's my mom's best friend. And on top of that, he's gay."

"Oh, phew," Dylan says. "You never know."

I make a face at him. "Uh, yeah, you do."

He laughs and is bending over holding his stomach. "Seriously, that was, like the best reaction ever. In the history of time. Ever. I was totally just fucking with you. Someone already told me he was like your uncle of something."

I can't help it I reach out and give him a light punch on his shoulder. "Not funny."

He's doubled over laughing still. "It's funny, all right."

And I think, *oh shit, he was asking about me.*

Just then the rest of his posse from the first night I met him comes over. "Hey," they say.

"Hey," I say back.

"Dylan. We're gonna bail now to check out that new band at The Viper Room. You in?"

He looks at me. I stare back.

"Give me a second," he says. They wander off.

"I know this is cheesy, but I think fate put us both here tonight."

"That's pretty cheesy," I say.

"You never answered my question."

"Which one? If Oscar was my boyfriend?"

"If you still have a boyfriend."

I shake my head. It makes me sad.

He smiles.

"Can we just hang out? Here, I mean. And just talk? Would that be okay?"

I exhale and think, why not? He has me laughing for the first time in weeks. It feels good.

I nod. He looks over at his friends who are off by the door and gives them a wave. They file out.

"So, Miss Kennedy from Brooklyn, who's your favorite band?"

"Wow, you go straight for the jugular," I say.

"Damn right."

"I'm really digging The Neighborhood."

He falls back in his chair and mimes a knife stabbing into his chest over and over. Then he stands and starts to walk away.

"Hey!" I say.

He turns. "Where you going?" I say.

"Might as well end it now before you break my heart anymore," he says as he sits back down.

"My turn," I say. "Yours?"

"The Beatles."

I whistle. "Impressive."

"Your turn."

"Okay," I say. "What is your favorite film. Be very, very careful with your answer. This could be a dealbreaker."

His eyes grow wide. "Can I make a call?"

I roll my eyes. "This is your opinion so no you can't make a call. There is no lifeline call here."

"Damn."

He puts his hand on his chin and starts mumbling to himself. "If I say *Star Wars*, she might get up and walk away from me thinking I'm a super nerd *or* she might hug me. If I say, *Beauty and the Beast*, she's going to think I'm gay. If I say *Saving Private Ryan*, she's going to think I'm some macho dude. If I say *Five Feet Apart*, she's going to think I'm actually a teenage girl..."

I laugh so hard I practically am crying. At the same time, I'm impressed. His taste in movies is pretty damn good.

I hold up my palm and he stops.

"What?" he says.

"You're out of time. Give it up."

"Just one?"

"Just one."

"Okay. I'm going to have to say. Starwarsbeautyandthebeastsavingprivateryanfivefeetapart."

I'm dying. I have tears rolling down my cheeks now.

When I catch my breath, I say, "You're telling me you're an effeminate, war mongering, nerd, pervert?"

"Yeah," he says nodding his head fervently. "Basically."

I squint my eyes and put my finger on my chin as if I'm thinking and then I say, "Well you're lucky you said the last one."

"Five Feet Apart?"

I smile. "It's my favorite," I say. "It's not high art, but I love it so much."

His grin is irresistible. "Mine too."

"Well there you have it," I say.

"I have an idea," he says. "Want to start a company with me? It will be like Match.com except we make people say their favorite movies?"

"Totally."

Then there's awkward silence.

"You dig movies, then?" he asks.

I nod. "I'm going to study film in college."

"Cool. Do you have anything I can see? That you've made?"

I think about my autobiography and shake my head.

"Not yet."

"But soon?"

I smile. "Maybe."

Then he grabs his phone and after a few seconds looks up. "You're on TikTok, right?"

I wince. "Oh, god, don't watch those videos."

"Too late," he says laughing. "I found you a long time ago on TikTok."

I moan.

"You're damn funny."

"Haha."

Then it's silent again. I look around. I was having so much fun I didn't realize that the crowd has thinned and there are very few people still on the rooftop. Oscar is sitting with a small group by a fire pit.

I stand. "I should probably go now," I say. "I think Oscar has an early call."

He stands, too. "I've got an early day tomorrow."

I raise an eyebrow. "You're such a jetsetter."

"I'm going home for Easter," he says. "But not until tomorrow night. In the morning, I'm in the studio for a few hours."

"Where's home?"

"Chicago."

"Cool. Do you have a big family?"

"Yes," he says and his voice lights up. "I'm the oldest. I've got a bunch of annoying little shit siblings."

He's smiling.

"Fun."

"Yeah," he says. "I can't wait to see everyone. I miss them. I also have like twenty cousins. We all go to my grandma's house for Easter."

"That sounds really great," I say. I feel a mixture of jealousy and happiness for him. It's a weird feeling. It sounds so perfect. Big family in Chicago. His life seems so normal. Well, except for jet setting off on tour and having screaming fan girls and people asking for autographs part.

"Can I see you when I get back?" he says. "Next week."

"I don't know."

"That's not a 'no,' right?"

"It's not a no," I say. "But it's not a yes, either."

"So, you're telling me I have a chance?"

"*Dumb & Dumber*," I say.

He winks and then leans over and kisses me. It's soft and warm and short and sweet. And I melt a little inside.

He pulls back immediately. "Thank you for hanging with me tonight," he says. "I seriously haven't had this much fun in a long time."

"Oh sure. Standing on stage with thousands of girls screaming and cheering as you sing?"

"Well," he says. "I mean besides that. I mean that's pretty hard to beat."

I laugh. "I like your honesty."

He tilts his head and looks at me so intently I can feel myself blush.

"It's great, really it is, but it's not the same as this."

We're at the door now. He pauses. Oscar is inside the lobby area waiting at the elevator holding the door open.

"I better go." I try to change the subject. "I'm glad I ran into you. I haven't laughed this hard for a very long time. I needed that."

Concern crosses his face and I look down, embarrassed that I've revealed so much.

"I think there's only one conclusion that you can come to," he says.

I look up. "Oh, yeah, what's that?"

"That I'm good for you."

I smile. But don't answer. Maybe he's right.

It's only after I'm home in bed that I think of Hunter and wonder what he's doing.

21

The next day we all pile into my minivan so I can drive us to Magic Mountain.

It's an unbearably hot day. Even the mist that sprays out from pipes onto people in line is not enough. We're baking in the hot sun. All of us wore shorts and small tops and soon our cheeks and shoulders are turning pink. Coral offers to go buy sunscreen at the gift shop.

When she returns, we all slather on thick white goo and laugh at ourselves. After going through the haunted house, which is cool and dark, thank God, it's time to get in line for the roller coaster. One of several there.

"I'll sit this out," I say.

"You sure?" Emma asks.

"Positive," I say. "I don't really feel like barfing up the eight-dollar water I just drank."

"Cool."

"See you in three hours," I say. I'm only half joking. They probably will be gone for at least an hour and a half. The entire world thought today would be a great day to go to Magic Mountain, apparently.

I find a spot in the shade. I cross my legs in some grass under a tree and scroll my phone.

Dylan snapped me at three this morning. It's four in the afternoon so I figure I've waited a suitable time to not appear desperate and open his snap.

I can't help it. I smile. It's a picture of him holding up a DVD of *Five Feet Apart*. It looks like he's in his bedroom. He has a sheepish grin on his face.

I angle my body so the roller coaster is in the background behind me and take a picture of myself, snapping it back to him.

He snaps me back instantly. All the rules of not being a dork require me to wait several hours before replying, but I think, 'Fuck it,' and open it.

He's in a recording studio with a huge microphone in front of his face. He's so cute.

I'm tempted to Snap him back immediately, but once was bad enough. Now he knows, or at least thinks, that I like him.

I blew it.

I instantly feel guilty. Hunter has my heart and that's all there is to it. I can't help how I feel—attracted and happy to be around Dylan and crazy about Hunter. It sucks.

I won't snap Dylan back again.

At least not until I know what my relationship status with Hunter is. Right now, that's not possible.

22

On Easter, I Facetime my mom. She's moving out here in two weeks. I can't wait.

Oscar and I go to some fancy restaurant in Hollywood for Easter brunch.

It's weird. It doesn't feel like Easter at all. Usually my mom bakes a ham and makes mashed potatoes and gravy and when my grandma was alive, she would come over. It wasn't a big deal, but it was always nice.

I've never heard of anyone going to brunch for Easter, but the place is packed. I guess it's a Hollywood thing.

Oscar explains it once our order comes. "L.A. is all transplants, you know," he says between bites of the thickest, most decadent French toast I've ever seen. "Most people aren't from here, so we create our own traditions."

Christmas was the same. Small tree. Big party with Oscar's friends over. That was it. No church. No big home cooked meal. It's all good, though.

Anything is better than the previous holidays, though, when my mom and dad both drank too much and fought all day. I don't remember any physical violence on those days but then again, I was hiding out in my room anyway, so who knows.

The week after Easter is spring break so I sleep in and watch movies all day. Paige and the rest of Hunter's family go to Palm Springs. Coral and a cousin fly to Ft. Lauderdale and Emma spends the whole time making college visits.

I know I should be doing school work or filming during the time off, but I just don't want to do jack shit.

One day Oscar knocks on my room when I'm still in bed at three.

He comes in and sits on the edge of my bed.

"Hey there," he says.

I sit up, worried something is wrong.

"You've been sleeping a lot lately," he says. "Which is totally cool, I mean, God knows I slept my way through my teen years. But I can't help but worry."

I frown. "Worry, why?"

He looks down. "I think you might be depressed."

I don't have anything to say. I stare off at the wall past him and think about it. I shrug.

"Am I totally off base?" he says.

I shake my head and look down. And then I blow air out loudly. "Maybe."

"You've been through a hell of a lot, girl."

I nod. Tears prick at my eyelids. I don't want to cry.

"That therapist you saw last fall seems cool."

"She is."

"That's always an option."

I look up at him. "Okay."

He leaves and gently shuts the door behind him.

I blink and think about what he's said. Shit. He's right. I'm depressed. I lay back down and think about it. It makes sense.

THE THERAPIST SQUEEZES me in on Friday before break is over.

I tell her everything that has happened since I last saw her.

When it comes to my break up with Hunter, I hesitate.

She notices. The pen in her hand pauses midair and she looks over at me.

I can feel tears dripping down my face. Fuck.

"I lost my shit," I say. And I tell her what I did.

She scribbles for a few seconds and then looks up at me. When she sees my face, she hands me a box of tissue. I wipe my tears and blow my nose.

"Thank you for sharing that with me," she says.

I nod and sniff.

"I know one thing we spoke about last time was your fear that you would turn out like your dad."

I inwardly cringe hearing her say this.

"I have some thoughts about this," she says. "I think that your anger has less to do with some genetic predisposition and more to do with you feeling depressed."

I make a face. "I think I need to take anger management classes or something." I'm not sure what the *something* is, but I know the court ordered my dad to do that. So, I probably need it, too.

"Let's go deeper for a second. Hear me out," she says with a smile. "Most of the time anger is the outward expression of another emotion we aren't dealing with."

I've heard that before.

"You think there are other things I'm not dealing with? Other emotions?"

"I don't know," she says. "I just want you to consider that."

"Okay," I say.

"For instance, when you think of your parents and how you felt then and how you feel now what is the predominant emotion?"

I swallow. "Sad."

"That would make sense."

"But, also, angry."

"That makes sense, as well."

"Helpless," I say, realizing that this is true, but not sure it's an emotion.

She glances down at her watch. "Our time is up but if you want I'd love to meet again next week. However, I want to be honest with you, I think we need to focus on your anger and its underlying root cause of depression."

few days after Easter I get a letter in the mail. It's weird nobody writes letters anymore, right?

It's from Hunter.

I rip it open in my room.

"I have so much to say, but the most important two things are that I love you and I'm so sorry."

He goes on to say he's not great at writing, but that he's been fooling around with his cell phone and made a video for me.

"I can't upload it until Sunday. My online privileges are limited. I can't even be online on my phone or text or anything in case you are wondering why you haven't heard from me. I mean, I could, but it was part of the agreement I signed and I want to follow the rules."

I have been wondering. And the relief that fills me in hearing from him proves that he still has hold of my heart.

The letter is short, but means the world to me. He signs it. "All my love. Forever." And he drew interlocking hearts with birds. I never even knew could draw. I never knew he was such a romantic.

I count the days until Sunday. That morning, I'm up early and checking my email every few minutes it seems.

Finally, shortly after noon, his email appears. It has a link to a YouTube video. "Don't worry," he writes. "The video is set to private."

Heart pounding, I click on it.

It's a close up of Hunter. He adjusts the camera and then leans back. He's in a bare bedroom with a twin bed with white sheets behind him.

"Kennedy, it's me. I vowed to send this to you without censoring it, so it would be like I was telling you this in person. I need you to see me raw and unedited. It's the only way I can prove to you that I'm worth your time."

He clears his throat and looks down.

"I want to make amends to you. I seriously betrayed your trust in me and I don't expect you to forgive me, but here goes—I'm so sorry. I hurt you. And that's the worst feeling in the world. So much of my life has just been shit. I mean, yeah, you're thinking, poor rich kid, life is so rough."

He looks away and swallows then turns back. "But you know what I mean. I never shared all of myself with anyone until you. Because you're good and kind and you get me. I mean, you really get me. I've never been more myself since I met you. That sounds weird. What I mean is when I met you I finally could be myself. I could act the way I felt inside. And you loved me for it even more. I didn't have to walk around like a dick anymore. Okay. That's a lie. I still walk around like a hardass, but the thing is you see right fucking through me."

I wipe away a tear. It's true. There is so much more to him than what's on the outside.

He continues. "And when my mom came back into my life, that real me, the part of me you brought out? That part of me fucking ran for the hills. I mean like this," he says and snaps his finger. "Because seeing my mom fucking sucked. I mean, all I could do was put up that wall again, that one from when I was little. And even though you climbed that wall, as soon as I saw my mom, I took you and tossed you right back over that wall and then put barbed wire up on top to keep you out again."

He looks over his shoulder and then back at the camera. "Hold on," he says. "They're calling me. I'll be back." His finger reaches out and the screen goes black for a second. Then he comes back on this time his hair is wet and he has on different clothes now, a dark green T-shirt.

"Back at you," he says. "I watched what I recorded already and it seems kind of vague, right? But what I'm trying to say is I realize now I pushed you away, hung out with Ava, and drank and did drugs to make sure you would break up with me." He winces. "Pretty fucked up, huh?"

"Yes!" I say feeling my anger surge.

"Totally the coward way out," he says. "And even if it means I've lost you forever, I'm incredibly grateful that I'm in this place. It has changed my life. For starters, it made me realize why I did what I did to you." He makes a face. "Okay, that couldn't have sounded more selfish, but what I mean is that I needed to know this. I needed to know that every asshole thing I've done in my life is because I'm a big fucking coward afraid to get hurt. And now that I know I can do better. Even if you don't forgive me and give me a chance to show you, I needed all this to happen."

I'm crying now. Because I don't know if I want to forgive him or want to give him a chance to show me. I really don't know.

"Okay, one more thing that is pretty important for me to share, but again totally self-serving. I mean, I'm not stupid, Kennedy, I know even my apology to you is selfish. But here goes. I've been judging the fuck out of my mom my entire life. I've been angry at her for not being strong enough to say no to her addictions and yes to me and her family," he says. "It took this happening to me to realize what it feels like and how hard it must be for her. She has her own demons to deal with. I didn't realize this. I was just a kid so I didn't know." His voice chokes up at the last sentence.

Then he reaches out and clicks off the video and I realize it's because he doesn't want me to see him cry.

Then he's back.

"I have been spending time with my mom here." His voice falters again and he closes his mouth for a second. "It's been crazy. We've both been doing some healing. It's no excuse, and she says it's no excuse, but she told me some stuff about her childhood and how fucked up it was and that maybe that's why she became an addict."

He exhales loudly. "Okay. That's it. That's my long ass video confession apology to you. I hope one day you can forgive me. If you think you might, I hope you might come see me on visiting day in two weeks. It's May 1. A Saturday. I'll put you on the list. If you don't come, it's okay. Really, it is."

Then the screen goes black.

I sit back. *Well, that was a lot of fucking shit to absorb*, I think.

I don't know if I'm going to go see him or not.

I don't trust myself to write him back by email. Instead, just to show I saw the video, I hit the thumbs up button under the video.

That night I'm already in bed when I get a frantic call from Paige. She's crying. I sit up straight in bed. Me and my friends never call. We text. We Snap. We DM. We don't call.

"Can you come over?"

"I thought you were in Palm Springs?"

"I'm back."

I glance at the clock in the dark. It says two in the morning. "Be there in ten."

I pull on a hoodie over my tee-shirt and leggings and slip on my flip flops. At the last minute, I write Oscar a note and leave it on the kitchen counter. "Paige needs me. At her house."

I know Oscar will understand. But I don't want him to worry if he looks for me and I'm not home.

As soon as I pull up, Paige comes out her front door. She's at my van.

"Let's go to the beach."

"Okay."

She hops in and doesn't talk until we get to the parking lot at the beach about a mile away.

I don't push her. She stares straight ahead out the front window.

We get out and I follow her down to the water. She sits so the waves lap her feet.

I sit beside her, close enough that we touch.

She leans over then and buries her face in my shoulder. "I'm pregnant."

I close my eyes. "Are you sure?"

She hesitates.

"Did you take a pregnancy test?" I ask.

She shakes her head. "But I'm late. I've never been late. Ever."

"Okay," I say. "But you don't know for sure."

"Greg thinks we should have it."

I feel sick. "What about college?"

Paige is the smartest one out of all of us. She got into Stanford.

"He says we could live off campus and have the baby."

I don't say anything. I think that's a huge mistake. But I'm not the one pregnant.

Shortly after Hunter and I had sex for the first time—using a condom—I went and got on the pill. And until he got tested for STDs, I still made him wear a condom.

But no protection, at all? No way. I know I'm not ready to be a mother anytime soon.

And I don't think Paige is, either.

She looks at me because I never responded to her comment about college with a baby. I think I owe her my honest thoughts, in a tactful way.

"It can be done," I say carefully. "But it would be really, really fucking hard."

Paige bursts into tears. "I know."

I hug her for a few minutes. Then she draws back and stares out at the water.

"Paige," I say. "You told me what Greg thinks, but you never have said what you think."

She nods. "I don't want a baby. I don't want to marry Greg. But I also don't want to have an abortion. And I don't want to break up with him. I just want everything to stay the same."

I exhale. "Okay. I think the first thing we have to do is go get a pregnancy test."

"Okay."

I'm slightly annoyed that Greg didn't insist on this first off. He's already making plans. I get that he was probably trying to comfort her, but making sure she's pregnant is the first step.

I stand and hold out my hand. "Come on. We're hitting the all-night drug store."

Armed with two pregnancy tests we return to her house just as the sky is lightening in the east.

Paige disappears into her en suite bathroom while I sit on her love seat.

After a few minutes, I hear her crying and don't know if they are happy or sad tears.

When she comes out, she puts out her hand for the second test. I hand it to her. Her face is red and puffy and her face is expressionless. I don't ask.

After a few more minutes, she comes back out.

"Both positive."

I try not to react, but she must see the look on my face because she says, "I know. Now what?"

She is looking at me like I have all the answers.

"That's up to you, Paige."

She closes her eyes. "I have to tell Greg it's for sure. But later. I'm so tired." She yawns and puts her head on my shoulder. Soon she's asleep. And not long after, I lean back and sleep, too.

Someone clearing a throat loudly wakes me.

I look up to see a man I've only seen in photos. Hunter's dad. He's good looking in an old guy way with blue eyes and dark hair and a nice suit.

"Ladies, you're going to be late for school."

Paige sits up with a jerk. "Oh no."

I stare at Hunter's dad. He's been a somewhat mythical figure. A famous director but also the dad of the man I love. As soon as I think this I realize it's true. I still love Hunter.

Paige shuffles off to the bathroom. He looks at me and raises his eyebrow.

"I'm Kennedy," I say, suddenly nervous.

He pauses and tilts his head, examining me.

"I'm Brock West.."

Before we can talk more Paige comes back, dressed in leggings and an oversized sweatshirt. Her hair is pulled back in a ponytail.

I jump up. "I can be ready in ten."

"Have a good day, ladies," Hunter's dad says and leaves.

Paige and I pull into school a few minutes later and hurry to our separate classes. I text her during the break.

"Lunch?"

"Meeting Greg."

"Text me deets later."

She gives my message the thumbs up.

At lunch with Emma and Coral, I feel guilty as if I'm hiding something, which I sort of am. But it's not my business to tell them about Paige. It sucks though.

After school, I still haven't heard from Paige. I finally call her.

It goes straight to voice mail.

I've been home about an hour and I'm sitting at the kitchen counter working on chemistry when she texts. "I'm here."

I open the front door and she's standing there with red eyes and a puffy face. I just reach over and hug her.

Inside, she goes straight to the refrigerator and opens it. I'm surprised. Oscar wouldn't care but it's weird to see her make herself at home. She takes out a carton of yogurt, some orange juice, a hunk of salami and some hardboiled eggs. Then she turns to me and raises an eyebrow.

"Yeah," I say. "Eat as much as you want."

"That's how I knew for sure I was pregnant," she says. "If more than two hours pass without food, I want to murder anyone who looks at me."

"Well, by all means, then, eat," I say.

I watch her pop one boiled egg in her mouth and then another. She finishes some salami and a dish of yogurt and slurps down some orange juice before she opens the cupboard and takes out some kale chips.

"Jesus, you guys eat too healthy around here," she says.

I watch, mesmerized, as she eats half the bag of kale chips and then goes and slumps on the couch.

"You done?"

She glares at me.

"Sorry. How did it go?"

"We broke up."

"Holy shit."

"He says it's his baby and he says I have to have it and I said I don't have to do anything and it's my body."

"Whoa."

"Yeah, no shit, right?" she says and leans her head back. "I'm so fucking tired. All I want to do is sleep. I read that's normal too right now."

I think about what she said. It sounds so complicated. I mean, how much say does Greg have? It *is* her body. It makes my head spin thinking about it.

And then she asks, "What do you think?"

I exhale and say, "I think it really sucks to be you right now, but that I trust you will make the best decision for you."

"Thanks," she says. "You sound like a mom."

"Are you going to tell your mom?"

Paige shrugs. "I am probably going to have to. Depends."

I reach out and hold her hand. "I'm here to help in any way I can. You know that."

She nods.

"You gonna tell the girls?"

"Yes," she says. "Can you ask them to come over?"

"Of course," I say and grab my phone. I feel so helpless that I'm eager to take even the smallest action to help.

In the meantime, while we sit and wait for Coral and Emma, Paige's phone vibrates nonstop. She looks down at it every once in a while.

"Greg," she says once when I glance at her phone.

Coral and Emma are over within the hour.

Paige tells them everything, crying. They both hug her.

"What do you think?" Paige says when they pull back.

"It's your body, girl," Coral says. "Greg has every right to express what he wants but ultimately it's up to you."

Emma nods. "What about Stanford?"

It was what I kept thinking. Sure, all of Paige's plans to study genetics and then go to med school for pediatric oncology *could* still happen if she had a baby. But unlikely.

"What do I do?" Paige says.

Coral sits up. "You need to go see a doctor."

"Right now?"

Coral shakes her head. "Probably not right away, but soon. No matter what you decide, you know?"

Paige swallows and nods.

"I could give it up for adoption."

Just then there's a knock at the door.

I go to see who is there looking through the window. And then turn to Paige.

"Its Greg."

24

Damn Snapchat map is creepy.

Brought Greg right to my house. Good thing he's not a crazy stalker dude.

When Paige opens the door, he bursts into tears.

I glance over and they are hugging. I hear him say, "I'll do whatever you want, Paige. I'll support whatever you decide. I promise."

Then the door closes. We look out the window and they are leaning against Greg's Honda talking. It looks pretty deep.

"Who wants pizza?" I say, reaching for my phone. "Speak up if you want anchovies or forever hold your peace."

THE NEXT DAY I'm walking from lunch to my Spanish class when I get a DM on my Instagram account.

It's Dylan.

"Hey. I'm in town. Like in your 'hood. Don't you go to Pacific High? I had a lunch meeting at the pier and don't want to fight traffic back to the valley. Want to meet me for ice cream? My treat?"

I smile. For one second I think of Hunter. But right now, I need to be around someone who makes me laugh, not cry.

"I still have two more classes." I know it's not a yes or a no, but I hit send.

"I'm not going anywhere. So...is that a yes?"

"K."

"Meet me at the pier at 3?"

"K."

I should feel guilty. But the truth is Hunter and I are broken up. I don't know if I'm going to go see him or not. Maybe seeing Dylan will help me decide.

When I pull into the parking lot near the pier, my windows are down and I'm blasting the music. It's the perfect L.A. day. The kind of beach day I always dreamed about during cold and dark Brooklyn winters when Oscar would call my mom and talk about the weather.

It always seemed so glamorous. And now it's my life.

As soon as I step foot on the pier, Dylan pops in front of me and I jump. He bursts into laughter.

"Sorry," he says.

I'm laughing, too. Every interaction with Dylan is fun. It's light-hearted and fun and makes me feel good.

Most of my interactions with Hunter are so fucking intense they take my breath away. Even the first time we met, he made me spitting mad. There is no lukewarm when it comes to Hunter West.

And I don't know which way is the right way. I mean if I'm gauging what a relationship should be like based on my parents passionate, volatile marriage, then what I have with Hunter is the way it should be.

Maybe for the rest of the world, this easygoing feeling that I get with Dylan is the way it is supposed to be. I just don't know.

We spend the afternoon eating ice cream and talking about things that aren't super deep. After we walk the length of the pier and play some mini golf that has me laughing so hard I'm crying at Dylan's antics, we hit the beach.

We take off our shoes and walk in the wet sand.

Finally, we sit. Dylan is sweet. He takes off his zip up hoodie and puts in on the sand for me to sit on. Then he stares out at the water and says, "Kennedy, you didn't snap me back."

"I know."

He doesn't say anything.

"I've got some things I'm figuring out," I say.

"Fair enough."

"Thanks," I say. But he doesn't leave it at that.

He turns to me. "Is one of those things a boyfriend?"

I shrug. "I guess," I say. "I mean I don't technically have a boyfriend right now, but I do have an ex and I'm not sure where we stand or what's going to happen. So, it's not really fair to..."

He leans over and kisses me. I'm surprised but find myself responding. How did I ever think being with him was easygoing and platonic? My body is lighting up from his mouth. I'm reaching for him and we're on the sand now and he's on top of me and my hands are buried in his hair.

Then he kisses my neck and suddenly it's Hunter's mouth I'm groaning under and I push away and sit up suddenly. He sits up beside me and his chest is heaving.

"God, I'm sorry."

He laughs. "For what? For being fucking hot as hell? No apology necessary, believe me."

"No, for leading you on."

"Um, that wasn't leading me on. That was amazing. Probably good thing we stopped, though. Otherwise we would've been arrested for indecency."

"Yeah, I think you're right," I say and laugh.

I stand. "I better go."

He stands, too, and reaches for me. He kisses me again and this time he pulls back.

"Hey, Kennedy," he says in a low voice. "If, when you do figure things out, your ex-boyfriend isn't in the picture, I have big plans for us."

"Oh, really?"

"Oh, yeah. You have no idea."

"Are you trying to sweeten the pot? Like, if I'm with you all these cool things will happen?" I tease.

"Kennedy, there are some definite perks to dating a dude in a boy band."

I laugh. "No offense, but all I see are the cons."

"What?" he says, and seems shocked. "Like?"

"You're gone all the time on tour."

"Ugh."

"Every female between eight and fifty thinks you're hot and wants to date you."

"Ouch."

I sit there silently.

"So, basically two cons?" he says. "Not bad. I was expecting more."

"Give me time."

He walks me to my car and I'm surprisingly disappointed when he doesn't kiss me goodbye. He just smiles and says, "Hope you figure things out soon, Kennedy. Because I'm finding it really hard to say goodbye to you."

I swallow and shut my door.

I stop at the mall to pick up some new gym shorts and have a coffee. When I get home, Oscar throws open the door. "Well, well, Kennedy, looks like someone wanted to send you a pretty clear message."

I'm confused. But before I step inside I can smell them. Flowers. Dozens and dozens of pink roses on every surface of the downstairs. I open the card. It says, "Not even a perk. Just the way I roll."

I smile.

25

Dylan doesn't try to get ahold of me again and I don't Snap him. I know I should say thank you, but I'm just too confused to respond to him in any way right now. But that doesn't mean I don't think about him. A lot. I replay our last conversation and neither one of us talked about being in touch.

After a few days, I'm pretty sure he's lost interest. He should. He probably spent a lot of money on all those flowers and it was sort of a dick move for me not to thank him. It's okay, though. That will make it easier, but I don't like it.

Still, I think about him—and Hunter—all the time.

I know it's not fair. It feels like I'm leading two different boys on. But I'm not. I've made no promises to anyone.

Paige asks me to come with her to the clinic where they are going to verify she is pregnant and tell her how far along she is.

When I pick her up, she seems more like her old self.

"I thought Greg would want to take you," I say.

"I didn't tell him I made the appointment."

I don't say anything even though I think this isn't the healthiest way to have a relationship, especially if they end up being parents together. But it's not my business.

It's only when we are in the lobby that Paige starts to seem nervous.

"What's up?" I text her so all the other people in the lobby don't hear us. "You seem really nervous. It's going to be okay. No matter what."

"I don't feel pregnant anymore," she writes back.

"What?"

"I was barfing every morning and now it's stopped. Two days ago. And I'm not tired, either."

"I heard once you are past a certain point it does get all better."

"Yeah."

"Do you *want* this baby?"

I see her frown as she taps her phone. "I don't *not* want it. It's weird."

"Yeah."

When the doctor calls her name, I look up and raise an eyebrow to see if she wants me to come with her.

"I'll be fine," she says.

I'm so nervous waiting for her and I don't know why. I sneak looks at all the other people in the waiting room. There's an older woman with gray hair. There's a couple who look like they're in their thirties with a little kid running around. There's a girl who looks like she's a couple years older than me, maybe early twenties. They all avoid eye contact. I scroll TikTok with my earbuds on and try not to laugh out loud at some of the videos. Nobody except the little kid is laughing.

Forty minutes later the door opens and Paige comes out. She has a blank look on her face.

We hurry out to the car. I'm dying to ask her what's going on. Once she's put her seatbelt on, she turns to me.

"There was no heartbeat."

"Oh my God, Paige. I'm so sorry," I say. I don't know if I should say I'm sorry or not. This is so confusing.

"The doctor said if it looks like the...baby...doesn't come out on its own, I have to go in for a procedure."

"Oh my God," I say again.

She stares straight ahead.

I reach for her hand. "How do you feel?"

"Okay, I guess. Sad and relieved at the same time."

"That makes sense."

"And I'm going to break up with Greg."

"Whoa," I say pulling over to the side of the road. "What?"

"You can drive you know," she says.

"Um, I didn't want to crash."

"I guess this whole thing made me realize that I want to be single when I go to college. I'd thought maybe we could try the long-distance thing but I need to concentrate on school."

I pull back onto the road.

"What? Nothing to say?"

"I'm happy for you, Paige. I think you would've handled whatever a pregnancy brought your way, but it also is good to see you taking charge of your life and your future."

"Thanks," she says and looks down.

For a second, I offer to take her to ice cream to celebrate, but that's wrong, too. There's nothing to celebrate about a miscarriage. What I want to celebrate is that she has her plans for her life back, the plans that light her up.

Then she looks over at me. "I need to tell you something."

"Do I need to pull over again?"

"Prolly."

I pull into the parking lot of a coffee shop. My heart is pounding. I have a feeling I know what this is about but I'm not sure I want to hear it. It has to do with Hunter.

"You know why we went to Palm Springs for break, right?"

I wince. "I think so," I say. "Is it close to where Hunter is?"

She presses her lips together and nods. I'd suspected as much.

"We all went to see him on Tuesday."

"I thought his visiting day was coming up," I blurt out. Paige gives me a surprised look.

"Family can visit any afternoon."

"Okay."

"He's crazy about you, Kennedy."

I close my eyes. I don't want to cry. Paige reaches over and takes my hand.

"He's changed."

My eyes open. "Did I ever tell you my dad went to rehab?"

"Oh no."

"Yeah. Didn't work."

"I'm not saying Hunter will be different, but we met with one of the directors there and she said that because Hunter got help right away and because he's young, she doesn't see any reason why he should have the addiction problems his mother does."

I feel a wave of relief. But I still have a knot of anxiety in the pit of my stomach. "I really want to believe that."

"I know. Me too," Paige says.

"I suppose I should at least go see him."

"I think he'd like that a lot."

I swallow. "Okay."

26

And just like that it's the day I'm going to visit Hunter.

I wake early and try on every single item of clothing I own until I settle on the red dress that my friends bought me when I first moved here. I know Hunter likes me in red.

It's a little too girlie, so I wind a thick black velvet ribbon around my wrist several times until it looks like a thick cuff and fasten it with a safety pin. I also wear my black vans. I washed my hair last night so I brush it and straighten it and let it hang down my back. I line my eyes with deep kohl and then put on some lip gloss and head out the door before nine.

My first stop is to drive through for a large latte with whip.

Oscar offered to drive but I'm looking forward to cranking my music on the drive.

I should be there by the time visiting hours start at noon, even if I hit traffic.

It's Saturday morning so traffic is light and within an hour I've left the L.A. basin. in my rearview mirror. I made a playlist for the drive and called it "All the Feels."

It has some of my favorite songs from senior year, including "Sunflower" by Post Malone; "Reflections" by the Neighborhood; "This

Could Be Us" by Rae Sremmurd; and even "Legends" by JuiceWRLD, which is probably a bad idea since it's guaranteed to make me cry since he died way too young.

When Tame Impala's "The Less I know the Better" comes on, I roll down the window and let the wind whip my hair as I sing at the top of my lungs.

I don't know if it's the playlist or the caffeine or simply the excitement of seeing Hunter, but the music really hits me hard. I'm super happy and super sentimental at the same time. My mom is moving next week. I'm driving to see a boy I'm crazy about. And the sun is shining.

After a few songs like this, I roll up my window and crank the air on the minivan, but it barely keeps me cool. By the time I pull into Palm Springs, the caffeine has worn off, I'm sweaty, tired, and suddenly full of anxiety. I have twenty minutes before visiting hours start at noon.

I want to stop for an iced coffee, but first I need to make sure I can find the place. It's on the other side of town. I drive by slowly. It looks like a country club from the front. It looks like there's even a golf course and pool in the back surrounded by palm trees. Not too shabby. But I suppose Hunter's dad is rich so it makes sense.

I turn around and head back to town. I know that an iced coffee probably isn't going to help since I'm already so nervous, but I need it.

In the coffee shop bathroom, I blot my sweaty face and fix my makeup. It helps, but not much. I shrug. Hunter has seen me even worse.

Finally, it's time to go. I climb into the van, close my eyes, and take ten deep breaths, holding and then exhaling. It was something the therapist taught me. I don't know if it helps or not.

When I pull up to the facility, I park in a visitor's spot and before I can even open my door, Hunter is there. He flings open the door and grabs me in a hug, picking me up and burying his face in my hair. I hug him back just as tightly.

He sets me down and pulls back to look at my face. We both are grinning like idiots.

"Damn you are a sight for sore eyes," he says.

"Same."

He takes my hand. "Hope you're hungry. I made us a picnic lunch."

"Starved."

Instead of taking me inside, he takes me by the hand and leads me along a path that stretches along the far side of the buildings and ends up in the back near a pool area. People are in swimsuits everywhere. I sneak a look and am surprised to find a lot of really beautiful young women who look like models lying in lounge chairs.

"Rough crowd."

Hunter glances over. "Yeah. Every model or actress who has a drug problem ends up here sooner or later."

"You sure you want to be seen with me?" I tease. "Might hurt your game."

He stops dead in his tracks and I nearly bump into him even though he's holding my hand.

Facing me he lifts my chin. "Kennedy? You got nothing to worry about."

He's already turned away and tugging me by the hand. In a large grassy area to the right of the pool is a blanket spread under some trees. There's a picnic basket on it.

"Voila!" he says as we get there.

"Cool," I say. It's a little awkward.

He made sub sandwiches and there is fruit and cookies and it's so sweet.

We eat and laugh a little and talk about silly things.

After I lay down on my back with Hunter beside me. He pulls me over so my head is resting on his stomach and he is smoothing my hair. I feel like we're on a first date or something. But I have to admit I like it. For so long everything between me and Hunter has been so intense. It feels good just to laugh.

It makes me realize that that's what I loved most about being around Dylan. Just having fun. Even though I do really like him as a person. He's a really sweet guy. And not bad in the kissing department, either.

But he's not Hunter.

Lying there, staring up at the clouds through the tree branches, as his fingers comb out my hair, I look up at Hunter and know that Dylan never stood a chance.

And when Hunter leans down to give me an upside kiss—the first kiss we've had in months—I know that nobody could ever compete with Hunter West.

Nobody.

"I SHOULD'VE TOLD you to bring your suit," Hunter says. "It's really hot."

"I don't mind." It's sort of the truth. I wish my hair wasn't damp and sticking to my face, but it's fine.

"Want to go inside and see my room? It's a little cooler there."

"Sure."

He takes me by the hand and leads me off to a door. The place is like a resort. There's a table set up with fresh coffee carafes and platters of food and snacks. Everything looks really healthy.

A few people smile at us as we go down a hall and then he turns and uses a key card to unlock a door. It's a simple room with a desk and twin bed. He has a huge blown up photocopy of a picture of me taped to the wall. His desk is stacked with books and journals.

He glances up at the picture of me. "That's what has kept me sane."

"Huh?"

"At first, I was here for you."

"What?" I start to protest, but he holds up a palm.

"But it didn't take long for me to learn that you can't get clean and sober for someone else. You have to do it for you."

I nod. "My mom said something like that about my dad. He went to rehab." I let it sit there.

Hunter flinches. "It doesn't help everyone, I know."

I wait. He comes over and leads me to the bed, patting it. I sit. He sits beside me.

"I've been thinking a lot in here. That's one thing I have a lot of time to do," he says. "And here's what I think. I think we should decide whether it's worth giving it a shot. Together."

"It?"

"Me and you. This relationship. It sounds like we both want to stay here for school so we could be together...I want us to work, Kennedy. I miss you."

He looks down.

I reach for his hand and squeeze it and he continues.

"The way I figure it, we both have shit to deal with. We both have parents who fucked up. We both don't want to be like our parents, right?"

I nod.

"I'm not going to drink or do drugs anymore. I don't want it. I don't need it. You don't want to be like your dad. You're not going to. We don't have to repeat the cycle."

I can feel tears threatening. I sniff and nod.

"You know who told me that about not repeating the cycle?"

I shake my head.

He exhales loudly. "My mom."

He is tapping the floor with his foot. He's nervous. I squeeze his hand hard.

"Part of what I've been doing here is getting to know my mom. Learning to forgive her. She told me things. She told me it's up to me to break the cycle. I'm going to do it, Kennedy. I swear."

"I believe you." And I do.

He leans over and kisses me long and hard. Then he stands and goes to lock his door.

When he comes back he pushes me back on the bed and kisses me and then lifts my dress above my waist.

I'm gasping with pleasure when I say, "Are you sure this is okay?"

He snarls. "I don't care."

I laugh.

We end up just making out and holding one another. It feels right. And less risky in case someone knocks. I don't think I could be comfortable anyway. You can hear voices of people walking by in the hall outside. Awkward. Hunter turns on some music low and that helps. But when some people are having a full-on conversation right outside the door, I sit up.

"I should probably go soon," I say.

"Hey," he says. "Want to meet my mom? I know she really wants to meet you."

I don't have to think about it.

"Yeah."

Hunter's mom is outside by the pool. She's sitting at a table reading a book with a title about healing your inner child.

"Ma?" Hunter says and the way he says it makes my heart melt. His mom looks up and smiles. She takes off her reading glasses and stands. "Kennedy," she says and her face lights up with her smile. She's really pretty. Her cheeks are pink and her dark hair and dark eyes are warm and loving. She looks nothing like the woman I saw on Hollywood Boulevard.

I stick out my hand. "So nice to meet you, Mrs. West."

She takes my hand and holds it tight. "It's a pleasure," she says. "You can call me Elizabeth."

There is an awkward moment where nobody says anything and we all just stand there. I gesture at her book. "That looks interesting."

She smiles. "It is," she says and then sighs loudly. "You'd think at forty I wouldn't need to deal with things from my childhood, but I do."

"I bet everyone has things to deal with," I say. "I think you're lucky to deal with it at forty because I bet some people never deal with it."

I cringe inside at my words. Lucky? Lucky to be in rehab dealing with your addictions?

She tilts her head to look at me and my heart pounds. But then what she says surprises me. "You are wise beyond your years," she says. "Lucky is right. And you're also right, most people live and die and don't figure out some basic things that would make their whole life better, richer, more fulfilling."

Then she looks down. "My greatest hope is that Hunter finds out these things at his age. If he can learn what I failed to learn at his age, he's going to have an amazing life and do amazing things."

We both look over at Hunter and I swear it seems like he's blushing. He looks down at his boots and then back up. But doesn't say anything.

"He's pretty amazing right now," I finally say.

His mom lights up and then reaches over to tousle Hunter's hair. "That's a fact," she says.

He backs up grinning and says, "The hair, mom!"

"Like you spent hours fixing it," I say.

Hunter is known for his messy hair. It's super sexy. But just wakes up and it's hot like that.

I know that visiting hours are almost over so I say, "I better go. It was so nice to meet you."

"Same here." She smiles and it seems a little sad.

"I'll walk you to your car," Hunter says.

At the minivan, we both lean on the side of it. Luckily, I parked in the shade, so it's not blazing hot.

"When you do come home?" I ask.

"Two weeks."

"What about your mom?"

He shrugs. "She can leave anytime. I don't think she's ready yet. She said something about being clean and sober for six months. And my dad doesn't mind paying for it. He's really decent that way."

"I finally met him," I say.

Hunter turns to me. "And?"

"He seems nice."

"He's okay."

"I better go," I say.

Hunter reaches for me and kisses me long and hard. I close my eyes and melt into his embrace. It feels so natural to be held by him and to have his mouth on mine.

When he pulls back he looks me right in the eyes. "Are we good?"

I smile. "Yeah."

His smile is blinding. "I'll see you soon."

I get in my car and he stands there with his hands shoved in his shorts watching me until I pull out. I can still see him standing there as I turn onto the highway.

27

The next day, after school, I'm thinking of Dylan.

It feels awkward, but it's only fair to text him instead of just leaving him hanging. If he still cares.

I send him this: "Hey, just was thinking about you and wanted to say first, thanks for the flowers. You are crazy and sweet. And I need to tell you that I finally figured out some things...I'm back with my boyfriend. But wanted to let you know I think you are amazing and I'm glad I got to know you. I hope you get everything you ever want in life."

He immediately replies. "Did you marry him?"

I make a face and reply. "Um, no."

"Well then you don't need to wish me a great life, Kennedy. You're what? Seventeen? Eighteen at the most? Unless you plan on marrying this guy, I pretty much figure I still have a chance. Hit me up when you're on the market again."

I'm both flattered and furious, most mostly furious.

"On the market again? You're fucking joking, right?" I hit send even though I realize tone is not conveyed well by text. But I don't have to worry because he writes back with an emoji laughing so hard it has tears.

"You're right. Totally lame," he writes. "Take two. Dear Kennedy, if you ever find yourself single again (unlikely, I know) please know there is one boy out there who is waiting for the day he hears from you again."

I stare at it. And close my eyes.

Damn, you're good, Dylan.

I'm at a loss what to say after that so I just send him a thumbs up.

I wait, but luckily, he doesn't answer. I exhale and put my phone down.

Maybe in another life.

28

I'm so excited. Today is the day my mom is coming.

Oscar and I spent a day shopping for the basement suite so it will be decorated and have everything my mom needs when she comes.

We buy bedding in her favorite colors: ivory and gray and I even stock the bathroom with some of her favorite products. I know she's moving out on the plane with only two suitcases, so I figure she's nearly starting from scratch.

Oscar is swinging by the airport to get her after work at the studio. I want to go too, but driving to the airport and during rush hour would be insane so I wait at home and pace.

By the time, she walks in—after extensive hugs and hand holding —she cries when she sees the basement.

Score.

There's a basket of fresh fruit and chocolate and a bottle of wine with a small card that says, "Welcome Home."

We even bought some cute clothes to put in the closet—a fancy black cocktail dress, a cute tracksuit, and a black bikini.

When she stops crying and hugging us, she flops on the bed and spreads out, smiling.

Then she sits up.

"This is possibly the nicest thing anyone has ever done for me in my life."

I'm overcome with sadness that I try to hide by smiling. Because I realize it's true. She's always done for everybody else. She's never done anything for herself. And my dad, he may have been good to her at one time, but I doubt he ever treated her the way she deserved to be treated.

Oscar ordered fancy food from a local place to be delivered and we all have wine. My mom says it's okay for me to have a glass. I'd set the table with linens and silverware and we eat by candlelight with the French doors thrown open to the warm night and the smell of the ocean coming in on the breeze.

We sit around the table and talk for hours. I fill her in on every little thing.

She just holds my hand and listens as if I'm telling her the most important secret in the world. And then she says, "I'm so proud of you, Kennedy."

I vow not to cry.

"And I'm so glad to be here," she says. "This is like a dream come true."

Then she yawns.

"Oh my God, mom, it's three hours later in New York. You must be exhausted," I say.

"Go to bed," Oscar says and kisses her forehead. "And sleep in. I don't want to see either one of you until eleven and then I want you in a cute dress because I'm taking you to the hottest new brunch spot in L.A. It took some major favors for me to pull a reservation."

He walks out and I walk over and hug my mom. She pulls me tight. I'm crying and I don't care.

"I missed you so much," I say.

"Me, too, honey."

29

I spend the next few days just with my mom and then it's the day that Hunter is supposed to be home. I'm a nervous wreck.

He texts me around noon.

"I'm sprung."

"Can't wait to see you."

"Having dinner with my family tonight, but can I come over after?" he says.

"Yes, please."

I spend the day anxiously awaiting. My mother and Oscar are car hunting.

Unlike New York, she's going to need a car if she has a job in L.A. Public transportation is not going to cut it.

After we have dinner on the patio, eating fish tacos that Oscar grilled, I tell them that Hunter is home.

My mom smiles. "That's great, honey." But then she frowns. "Are you okay with everything now?"

"I think so," I say.

"That's great, honey," she says. I don't know why, but I feel guilty. I know she wishes my dad would've left rehab reformed.

"I'm going to see him later if that's okay," I say.

My mom puts down her napkin. "You are a senior in high school and so responsible and mature that I don't think you need to ask my permission for things like that," she says. "The only thing I would ask is if you are going to be out super late maybe leave a note or text so I don't wake and worry about where you are or if you are hurt somewhere."

"That's fair," I say.

Oscar is blushing. "I pretty much let her do whatever the hell she wanted."

My mom bursts into laughter. "Of course, you did,"

HUNTER CALLS me at eight that night. I've been sitting there ready for his call. My makeup is done and I have on what I think is cute, but casual clothes—sweatpants and a cute top.

I'm surprised when my phone rings.

"Hey," he says in a low rumble.

"Hey, yourself," I suddenly wish he would call me all the time. His voice on the phone is sexy.

"I'm dying to see you but my dad made this into this big fucking dinner deal with a bunch of people from the movie he's working on. It has really nothing to do with me and everything to do with him hosting a big fucking party. I totally thought I could sneak out but I don't know."

I hear loud voices in the background. Then I hear his dad calling his name.

"Want me to call if it ends early, like before ten?"

"Sure," I say. "But don't worry about it. I'll see you tomorrow, right?"

"Yeah. For sure. You could not keep me away."

"Night," I say. I hang up feeling disappointed. But it's not his fault. I mean, he could sneak off, but I know his dad has a lot of power over him. He's talked about that before and how he has a hard time saying no to his dad.

I shower, brush my teeth and wash my face, and then crawl into bed in my comfiest flannel pajama pants and softest tee-shirt. But I can't sleep. I reach for my phone and Snap my friends Paige.

Coral and Paige snap back. Emma is probably asleep. Coral is in her room.

Paige is in her living room. She makes a goofy face. There is a crowd of people behind her. The party with the movie people. As I think this, I catch sight of his dark head in the background of the photo. I blow up the picture. It's fuzzy, but clear enough for me to see his head is bowed close to that of a girl with blonde hair. They're sitting together on the couch.

Jealousy spikes through me. He should be with me. My stomach hurts. But I reassure myself that everything is fine. That he loves me. That he can talk to any girls he wants. That I don't want to be that sort of jealous girlfriend. That's not my style.

Even so, it makes me feel bad. I miss him. He canceled because he claims his dad is making him stay for the party, but there he is apparently having a good time with a girl. My thoughts are poison. Toxic.

To distract myself I click on TikTok. The first video features a song by Dylan's band. It makes me smile. Then, even though I know it's wrong, I search for him on Instagram. When I find his page, I see he has followed me. I am rarely on Instagram so I didn't see this earlier.

I scroll through his feed. He's always laughing and goofing around with his band mates. There is only one picture that shows what he really does. He's standing on a stage with thousands of heads in front of him.

My finger hovers over the "Follow Back" button. And then I think of Hunter's head bowed close to that girl's head in conversation and I hit "Follow Back."

I set my phone down as if it burned me. Because I know I'm playing with fire.

30

The next morning I'm still asleep when I feel someone crawl into bed beside me and wrap their arms around me from behind. At first, I'm half asleep and when I feel lips on the back of my neck I moan in pleasure. But then I come fully awake and jump out of bed startled.

"Jesus Christ!"

It's Hunter.

"Hey, sleepyhead," he says. "Your mom and Oscar were just leaving and they let me in to wake you up."

"Oh, crap," I say and scramble to sit up. "I'm late for brunch."

"Nah. They're going to the grocery store or something. They said they'll be back in a few hours and then you guys are going to brunch"

I squint. "What time is it?"

"Eight."

I pull the pillow over my head. "Too early," I grunt. But then Hunter yanks it off me.

"Nice try."

I laugh. He knows I'm excited to see him. He goes in to kiss me and I jerk away.

"At least let me go brush my teeth."

I start for the bathroom when he says, "Those are some really sexy pajamas," he says. "I always did go for the Lumberjack look."

I roll my eyes.

After my teeth are brushed and face washed, I come back in. He's resting on one elbow smiling. His shirt is off. I look around horrified.

"Don't worry," he says. "We have at least an hour."

Even so, I stalk over to the odor and lock it.

As I make my way back to the bed, I walk slowly keeping my eyes on his as I tug my tee-shirt over my head and let it drop to the floor. Then standing in front of him near the bed with our eyes locked. I undo the drawstring on my oversized pajama pants and they drop to the floor. I stand before him in just a tiny silky slip of coral bikini bottoms.

He moans. "Jesus, Kennedy, you're so damn beautiful."

"Come show me," I say, beckoning him with a finger.

He is standing before me in seconds and then drops to his knees before me. Soon I feel his mouth on my belly and I close my eyes and give myself to Hunter.

It is only later, when we are both dressed sipping coffee on the patio overlooking the ocean that my doubts from the night before creep back in. I don't want to seem like a jealous girlfriend, but if I don't at least say something I know it's going to eat at me and the doubts will grow.

Without looking at him, I say, "How was the party last night?"

He shrugs. "It was cool," he shoots a quick glance at me. "But I would've rather been with you."

"It seemed pretty crowded."

He gives me an odd look.

"Oh," I say, "Paige snapped me. It looked crowded."

"Yeah. It was."

"Did you know anyone there," I ask.

"Yeah, a few people."

"Oh."

He turns now to face me. "Why all the questions? What's going on."

I shrug.

"Kennedy?"

"I just saw a picture of you talking to some blonde girl. That's all. It's no big deal."

He doesn't answer at first and my heart seems to skip a beat.

"Oh."

I wait and am suddenly anxious He clears his throat and I'm even more nervous.

"That was Natalie."

"Oh." I say and press my lips together tightly.

"She's an actress."

"She looks familiar. Has she been in anything I've seen?"

He blows out a puff of air and my heart clenches again.

"You might have seen her in Palm Springs."

I close my eyes. This is worse than I imagined.

"Did you invite her?"

"Oh, God no," Hunter says. "My dad did."

"Why?" I say and turn to look at him.

He shrugs. "I have no fucking clue. That's my dad for you. It's just how he is. When he has a party, it's always the hottest actors and directors and other people in the business. He's just like that."

"Oh."

Hunter reaches for my hand and laces his fingers through mine. "It might seem weird, I get it," he says. "But you need to know that you have nothing to worry about."

I nod, but keep my eyes facing the sea.

"Kennedy? Look at me."

I do and he leans over and kisses my brow so sweetly. Then he pulls back. "You are the only girl for me. Don't you know that by now?"

And suddenly, all my doubt and jealousy is gone.

I smile and crawl onto his lap facing him. I grab his head and pull him toward me until his mouth is on mine again. We kiss until I hear voices and a door slam and I jump off as fast as I can and am sitting beside him innocently when my mom and Oscar walk in.

It's great having Hunter back. At school, we are inseparable. He picks me up and drives me to school every day. He walks me to most classes and we eat lunch together at least twice a week. The rest of the time I eat with the girls and he hangs with Dex and Devin.

He had to drop film when he went into rehab. Most of his other classes gave him online assignments to allow him to catch up in time to graduate with the rest of our class. He seems really dedicated and we spend many nights studying until late.

On weekends, we either hang out and watch movies or go to the bonfires which are starting up again now that's its spring. Dex and Coral are still going strong so we also double date with them once in a while.

Paige and Emma join track and are busy with practice or meets every day after school.

Everything is going great.

My mom is searching for a job, but it's turning out to be tougher than she thought.

"I guess I didn't realize that being forty and not having worked for twenty years is a definite problem," she says one night at dinner.

Oscar nods. "Yeah, that's tough, but somebody out there is going to see how awesome you are and hire you. It just might take longer than we thought."

One day there's a moving truck next door.

"Damn," Oscar says. "I was hoping you guys would buy that house so we could be neighbors for life."

My mom and I laugh. Never in our wildest dreams could we afford that house. The next day I see a tall woman with reddish hair out on the deck of the house looking out at the ocean. Her hair is whipping in the wind. She looks so glamorous. I wonder if she's famous. I've gotten used to that in Los Angeles—famous people at every turn.

I'm lost in this thought when I realize she's turned and is staring at me. I am embarrassed to be caught spying on her so I halfheartedly raise my hand to wave. She stares at me for a second and then nods and disappears inside the house. Weird.

I wonder if, despite Oscar's joking, I could ever afford a house like that. I mean if I became a famous director like Hunter's dad, maybe.

My film project for this semester is nearly done. I turned in a slapstick comedy that I'm pretty proud of. I would never admit this to anyone, but it's inspired by my conversations with Dylan. There is something slapstick about how we interact. I sort of miss him, but now that I'm back with Hunter, I realize that nobody could ever compare.

I've been accepted to the USC film school. And scholarship money is there. All I need to do is get a job for the summer to pay the difference.

Oscar says that he's pretty sure he's going to get hired for Hunter's dad's film that starts next month and he'll lobby for me to be hired as an intern for the summer.

Even though it seems kind of awkward to work for Hunter's dad, it's going to be an epic experience.

Hunter's dad makes me nervous, though, for some strange reason. And sure enough, that weekend I know why.

It's a blazing hot day and Hunter coaxes me into coming over to his place to swim.

"Come on," he says. "My dad is going out of town and Paige and my mom are going into the valley to go shopping. I'm lonely. I want to swim and work on my tan."

"You're such a pretty boy," I say.

"I didn't hear you complain about my tan when we first met."

"You're right. You could use some sun."

"Harsh."

When I show up, Hunter is already in swim trunks and leads me out to the pool.

I pull off my sundress. Underneath, I'm wearing a white crocheted bikini which I know looks good against my own naturally olive skin.

Hunter immediately picks me up and jumps into the deep end of the pool holding onto me. When we surface, I'm gasping for air and pretend to be angry.

"Geez, trying to drown me?"

"Did you know I'm certified as a lifeguard?"

"What?"

"You think that's hot don't you?"

"Totally."

We get out and dry off in the baking sun. After a while, Hunter sneaks over where I'm lying on my stomach and dumps a bottle of water on my back. I scream and am chasing him around the pool vowing retaliation when I suddenly notice Hunter's dad standing in the open French doors watching us.

He's wearing a full suit even in the heat. We both freeze and he walks out to the pool area. His eyes flick over me and even though at the end of his quick appraisal he shoots me a smile, I can't help but feel that he has judged me and found me lacking.

It makes my mouth grow dry.

"Sorry to interrupt," he says, ignoring me again and looking at Hunter. "My plane leaves in two hours and I can't seem to find the notes I made on the script. Is there any chance you might have picked them up with your own papers last night?"

I'm trying to figure out what he's talking about and why Hunter might have the script or what his dad means by his own papers—homework? —when a harried looking maid rushes out.

"Mr. West? Mr. West? I found them. They were with the morning newspaper." She is an older woman with a kind smile she flashes on all of us.

His dad grins. "You are an angel, Margarita. I don't know what I would do without you."

"Let me think? You would have a messy house?" she says with a sparkle in her eye. "Miss your ride to the airport that is in the driveway?"

"Oh, God," he says and rushes inside after her.

It's odd. I would've expected him to say goodbye. At least to Hunter. I mean he is going out of town, right? It's a little weird, but I forget about it when Hunter loops his arm around my waist and pulls me over to a double-wide lounge chair.

"Lie down. I think your back needs some sunscreen."

"Oh, it does," I say.

31

One day Hunter and I go to the bookstore for fun. He's off in the science fiction section and I wander over to the self-help. I'm wondering if I should pick up a book that my therapist recommended for adult children of alcoholics. She says that I'm almost eighteen so she'd want me to read that over one about kids.

While I'm looking, I see the book that Hunter's mom was reading and pick it up. I start flipping through it and soon am sitting on the floor reading.

After a while Hunter texts me.

"Where you at?"

"Self-help."

Soon, he's by my side. When he sees what I'm reading, he doesn't say anything.

"It's pretty good," I say.

He doesn't answer.

But I buy it. Later that night I start to read it before bed.

The whole thing is good but I like what it says about the only way we can truly grow as people is to face our fears. There is a space to list our greatest fears. The author recommends we see if any of them are something we can confront. Some, like death, obviously aren't. But others, like fear of public speaking, can be addressed. She recommends we take baby steps.

I list my greatest fears: repeating my father's anger management and violent tendencies.

That is number one. I'm not sure how to confront that one.

Also on my list are spiders and roller coasters.

I look at the last one. Why roller coasters? It makes no sense.

On impulse, I reach for my phone and text Hunter. "Will you take me to the pier? I think I want to try riding a roller coaster again."

He texts back immediately. "You sure?"

"Positive."

"Is this the real Kennedy Conner?"

I ignore that and finally he texts back, "Cool."

32

I don't eat breakfast or lunch. I'm too nervous about riding a roller coaster later.

When Hunter picks me up he has the biggest grin.

"What?" I say.

"This is awesome. I'm going to start calling you Roller Coaster Girl."

"Please don't."

When we get to the Santa Monica Pier, I almost turn around and run back to the car. My hands are shaking. What the hell? It's such a stupid thing to be afraid of.

And then, standing at the foot of it and looking up it hits me. I know why I'm afraid. I'm suddenly a toddler again at Casino Pier in New Jersey. I'm holding my dad's hand and he's looking up at the roller coaster. And then suddenly he lets go of my hand and is gone.

I look around the crowd, frantic, but I don't see my dad. I'm scared and start to cry.

Then he's back at my side and holding me. "Pumpkin, it's okay. I'm so sorry. I saw something—someone doing something dangerous and I had to go help. I'm so sorry if you were scared."

He scoops me up in his arms and I cry even harder.

And just like that with this memory I want to cry.

For one, it's the dad of my childhood, the dad I loved and looked up to so much. And then it's also the realization that it's not the roller coaster I'm afraid of. It's just that I was afraid and now I've somehow associated that with the ride.

Hunter nudges me. "Hey? You good?"

I turn and smile at him. "I'm great. Let's do this."

"That's my girl," he says.

"Give me just one second," I say at the last minute and lean on the rail overlooking the water. Remembering my dad like this hits hard.

I suddenly realize that there is another thing on my list: I'm afraid of my dad. I'm afraid to see him. I'm afraid to trust him. I'm afraid to love him again. Because I'm afraid he will hurt me. Not physically, but emotionally.

That might be my biggest fear—above everything else. I close my eyes and with the heat of the sun on my face, realize that confronting my dad is going to be added to my list. And that I'm going to cross it off.

One by one, I will cross off the things I'm afraid of after I confront them. Today is just the beginning.

When I open my eyes, I take Hunter's hand and lead him to the line for the roller coaster. It takes us about fifteen minutes to get to the front.

When the car for us pulls up I climb in and sit down.

Hunter stands by the side of it until all the cars are filled and the roller coaster operator is waiting for us. He looks irritated.

"Get in or please move off the platform," he says.

Hunter ignores him and looks at me.

"Are you sure, Boots?"

I nod.

Only then does he get in, too.

The guy operating the ride rolls his eyes but comes by and checks the bar holding us in to make sure it's secure. Even though the guy is crabby I give him a grateful smile.

And then the ride starts.

I clutch Hunter's hand and he grips mine.

Then we are moving!

The cars crawl slowly up a steep incline and the clickety clack of the gears sounds like something awful going wrong but Hunter is looking at me and smiling so it must be normal.

Then we are at the summit and there is nothing but air before me.

in the distance is the ocean and I'm certain we are going to plunge right off the pier into the ocean and then sink to the depths.

We are about to die!

And then we are over the summit and soaring into what feels like space as the most blood curdling scream I've ever heard comes out of my own mouth. At the same time, an incredible jolt of adrenaline zips through me and I'm grinning so hard my mouth hurts and I'm laughing with sheer joy.

We go faster and faster, until my hair is blowing back and there is a curve that sends me careening into Hunter's shoulder.

Then with a heart wrenching lurch, we drop, but it's just a small drop this time, and my heart is in my throat and I'm screaming like a bloody fool and I'm laughing at the same time. A smile is plastered across my face. I'm holding Hunter's hand so tightly I'm sure I'm cutting off his circulation.

On a flat part, I sneak a glance over at Hunter and he looks back, grinning at me like an idiot. Then the ride climbs again and I am brave enough to look off to the side and see the amazing beauty of the beach and ocean and think that I've never been so happy in my life.

Hunter releases my hand and thrusts both of his arms up in the air right when we get to the highest peak. His hands are in fists and he looks at me.

I'm gripping the bar as if my life depends on it, because it probably does. But then when I see the sheer ecstasy on his face, I let go and throw both my arms into the air just as we crest the summit and plunge down.

When the ride comes to a stop I have tears streaming down my face.

Hunter looks over at me and his grin disappears.

I smile through my tears. And then I grab him and hold him tight and whisper in his ear.

"Thank you, Hunter West."

"Uh, okay," he says. "For making you bawl?"

"For being you. This might be the best day of my life."

He draws back laughing. "Does that mean you want to go again?"

I nod. "Hell, yeah, I do."

As long as Hunter is by my side I want to go again and again and again.

The End

To Be Continued ....

***

Want to read more Hunter and Kennedy?
Grab next book in the series, *The Mean Girl*.
***

I hope you enjoyed *The Good Girl*. If you want to be first to hear information on new books and sales, sign up for my newsletter
https://www.subscribepage.com/ashleyrosebooks
BONUS: If you've read *Raven* (AFTER meets PAPERTOWNS) and
"This generation's Outsiders."
You'll get the exclusive epilogue to that book so you can find out what happens to Raven & Hazel.
NOT AVAILABLE ANYWHERE ELSE
Remember, You'll also be the first to know when each book in the Pacific High Series is available!
https://www.subscribepage.com/ashleyrosebooks

Printed in Great Britain
by Amazon

22227480R00085